She'd expected to be watched, but electronic surveillance?

Now that Luke had his wife and child back home, he'd taken strong measures to keep them there.

"Will you allow my daughter and I out to go shopping?" Beth asked, knowing the answer before he replied.

Luke's eyes darkened. "No," he said flatly. "As I explained, you're free to leave the house whenever you wish—providing you're alone. Everybody here, even the cleaning help, knows that you are never allowed to go out of the house with Kristin, *our* daughter, unless I'm with you."

Beth's position in the household would be degrading at best, and at worst intolerable, but she refused to reveal her dismay. "Well, I guess that takes care of everything we have to say to each other," she said.

"Not everything," he said quietly. "But everything you're ready to hear right now."

D0036355

JASMINE CRESSWELL, who studied philosophy and history, met her future husband when she was assigned to the British embassy in Rio de Janeiro. Their frequent moves thereafter took them to eight different countries before they finally settled down in Denver, Colorado. She embarked on a career writing fiction, knowing that it was the one job she could take with her anywhere in the world, and she has been writing with increasing enjoyment ever since.

Books by Jasmine Cresswell

HARLEQUIN REGENCY ROMANCE
TRAITOR'S HEIR

These books may be available at your local bookseller.

Don't miss any of our special offers. Write to us at the following address for information on our newest releases.

Harlequin Reader Service
901 Fuhrmann Blvd., P.O. Box 1397, Buffalo, NY 14240
Canadian address: P.O. Box 2800, Postal Station A,
5170 Yonge St., Willowdale, Ont. M2N 6J3

JASMINE CRESSWELL

hunter's prey

Harlequin Books

TORONTO • NEW YORK • LONDON
AMSTERDAM • PARIS • SYDNEY • HAMBURG
STOCKHOLM • ATHENS • TOKYO • MILAN

Harlequin Presents first edition September 1986
ISBN 0-373-10913-X

Copyright © 1986 by Jasmine Cresswell. All rights reserved.
Philippine copyright 1986. Australian copyright 1986.
Cover illustration copyright © 1986 by Wes Lowe.
Except for use in any review, the reproduction or utilization of
this work in whole or in part in any form by any electronic,
mechanical or other means, now known or hereafter invented,
including xerography, photocopying and recording, or in any
information storage or retrieval system, is forbidden without
the permission of the publisher, Harlequin Enterprises Limited,
225 Duncan Mill Road, Don Mills, Ontario, Canada M3B 3K9.

All the characters in this book have no existence outside the
imagination of the author and have no relation whatsoever to
anyone bearing the same name or names. They are not even
distantly inspired by any individual known or unknown to the
author, and all incidents are pure invention.

The Harlequin trademarks, consisting of the words
HARLEQUIN PRESENTS and the portrayal of a Harlequin,
are trademarks of Harlequin Enterprises Limited and are
registered in the Canada Trade Marks Office; the portrayal
of a Harlequin is registered in the United States Patent
and Trademarks Office.

Printed in U.S.A

CHAPTER ONE

BETH HAD STARTED WORK at the supermarket in October, and since then, she had sometimes gone for several hours at a stretch without thinking of Luke. But today, for some reason, she couldn't get him out of her mind. Her fear was so strong she could taste it, a hard lump forming in her throat every time she swallowed. It required real physical effort to stay at the cash register and not simply take to her heels and run.

She finished bagging groceries for a young woman with two irritable toddlers in tow and reached for the next shopping cart. She recognized the old woman pushing it as a regular customer and smiled politely.

"Good morning, Mrs. Halloran, how are you today?"

"Fine, thanks. The sunshine's lovely for November, isn't it?"

"Yes," Beth agreed. "But we'd better make the most of it. The weathermen are predicting snow before the end of next week."

"Oh, you don't want to pay any attention to those TV weather forecasters! They predict snow every weekend once it gets this close to Thanksgiving. They like to make the skiers happy."

Beth laughed and made some suitable reply, although her conscious mind scarcely registered Mrs. Halloran's comments. Over the past twenty-seven months, she had become very proficient at answering people when her attention was light-years away from her actual surroundings.

She took a bunch of green onions out of the shopping cart and keyed in the pricing code. The hairs at the back of her neck prickled with an irrational, primitive sense of danger, and her hands weren't quite steady as she reached for the next item in the cart. She stroked a box of detergent over the scanner and looked warily around the giant supermarket.

The store was crowded with the usual assortment of Saturday-morning shoppers, mainly women, interspersed with a few teenagers and a scattering of men. She stared intently at the various men, but they looked just the way she would expect grocery shoppers to look on a late fall day in Colorado. Most wore jeans and thick sweaters, teamed with scuffed leather boots, and a couple wore Stetsons with dangling peacock feathers tucked in the brim.

None of them wore conservative three-piece business suits and starched white shirts. None of them was six foot two with raven-black hair and probing gray eyes. None of them looked intent on kidnapping her. None of them looked like one of Uncle Peppe's henchmen. And none of them looked even remotely like Luke Caine.

Beth drew in a deep breath. "That will be fifty-two dollars and four cents," she said, handing over a pen so that the customer could write out her check. "Do you need help to carry out your groceries, Mrs. Halloran?"

"No thanks, my dear. Fifty-two dollars doesn't buy enough to make my shopping bags heavy!"

"I'm afraid you're right." Although Beth produced another cheerful smile as she initialed the check and slipped it into the cash register, her stomach had started to churn so violently she was afraid she might be sick. She spotted one of the supervisors walking by and called out, her request low but urgent.

"Jill! Could you take charge here for a few minutes?"

The supervisor stepped over at once. "Of course. What's up, Beth? You look as if you've seen a ghost. Aren't you feeling well?"

"Not too good right at the moment, but I'll probably be fine in a few minutes. That's the trouble with being thin and pale." Beth edged out of her place behind the checkout counter, trying to make her voice sound as normal as possible. "I look half-dead even when I'm feeling terrific, and when I'm really sick I look as if I'm about ready for a trip to the funeral parlor."

"I wish I looked as good as you when I'm healthy, let alone when I'm sick," the supervisor said, positioning herself behind the cash register. "But take your coffee break anyway, Beth. Give yourself a full half hour to recover."

"Thanks, I really appreciate the help." Beth just managed not to run as she traversed the aisle leading to the staff exit. Her need to be out of the supermarket was overwhelming, and her instincts had been right too many times in the past couple of years to doubt them now. Like anybody on the run, she had honed her senses to scent danger, and she scented it today, just as she had in Pennsylvania and Ohio, just as she had in Indiana, Kansas and Nebraska. She was sure it was her instinctive awareness of when it was time to pack up and move that had kept her safe from Uncle Peppe. And from Luke.

She ran through the small staff room to the lockers. She dialed the combination on her padlock, feeling a sharp regret at the prospect of leaving Colorado so soon after her arrival. She had tried hard not to become attached to any community where she had lived during the past two years or so, but everything had worked out so well in Denver. Jessie, for example, would surely prove irreplaceable....

She grabbed her purse and jacket and headed for the back door, punching her time card in case the manager happened to be watching. Fortunately the supermarket was so large and remained open for so many hours each day that all the employees worked to individual schedules. Even if he saw her, the manager wasn't likely to wonder why she was leaving at 11:30 in the morning.

When she didn't return to her register, Jill would assume that she had felt so ill that she needed to go home, and with luck, everybody would be too busy to attempt to track her down until the next morning. By then, she would be out of the state.

The store owed her four days' wages, so she could soothe her guilty conscience with the knowledge she wasn't in debt to the supermarket. Her abrupt departure would inconvenience them, but at least it wasn't dishonest.

Beth pushed open the heavy swing doors of the staff exit. The daylight was momentarily blinding after the dimness of the corridor, and she closed her eyes for a moment before reaching into her pocket for her sunglasses. Denver was a mile above sea level, and at such a height the sun shone most of the year with a brilliance that was literally dazzling.

A shadow passed between her and the sun. Then a voice spoke softly.

"Hello, Beth. I've been waiting for you."

Her fingers froze into numbness and her sunglasses landed on the sidewalk with a dull crack.

"Luke!" she whispered.

He was just as she had remembered him. He hadn't changed at all in the past twenty-seven months. Tall, dark, conservatively dressed in a typical lawyer's suit of gray pinstripes, he still managed to look impossibly sexy. No wonder he always came across so well on television talk shows. For a wild moment she considered running back into the store and screaming for help, but she resisted the impulse, knowing that it would be useless. She would only make herself appear foolish, and in the end nothing would be changed. Luke would see to that. A politician to his aristocratic fingertips, he was accustomed to wooing hostile crowds. She had no hope that anybody would believe her frantic garbled tale once he started weaving his magic web of lies.

She bent down to retrieve her broken sunglasses and straightened slowly, shoving her hands deep inside her jacket pockets so that he wouldn't see them shaking.

"What do you want?" she asked. Her voice sounded unnaturally flat and overlaid with harshness.

"What do you think I want?" he responded laconically. "I want my child, of course."

She had known exactly what he was going to say, but actually hearing the words was such a shock that she reacted without conscious thought. She took to her heels and tore across the parking lot with all the speed blind panic could give her. He caught up with her before she had covered fifty yards. He grabbed the back of her jacket and swung her around to face him.

"Don't touch me," she hissed.

His eyes gazed at her with complete coldness and indifference. She noticed with a fleeting sense of puzzlement that they didn't even register dislike.

"We'll go to my car," he said coolly. "We can talk there without having you take flight every time I say something you don't want to hear."

"There's nothing you can say that I do want to hear. And I have nothing to say to you."

Ignoring her remarks, he marched her alongside him to a maroon Buick Regal parked near the front entrance of the store.

"I went to your apartment this morning before I came here," he said, unlocking the car. "But there was nobody in the building. There weren't even any neighbors around for me to question."

"You have absolutely no right to question my neighbors! How dare you force your way back into my life? You have no right to go to my apartment building!"

"No right?" He smiled bitterly. "You've hidden my child from me for two years. I'm a father and I don't even know my child's name. I don't even know if my child is a boy or a girl. If you're wise, Beth, you won't talk to me about rights. My self-control is a little fragile just now, and I'm not likely to be very receptive to that sort of discussion."

"You have no rights," she repeated through clenched teeth. "You have no rights where my child is concerned."

"Fortunately the law says otherwise. Thanks to the fact that my lawyers couldn't find you, I was never able to serve you with divorce papers. Therefore you still happen to be my wife. A trivial fact to both of us, maybe, but legally significant nonetheless."

"I won't allow you to see . . . my child," Beth said. "I'll call the police if you attempt to see . . . it."

For a moment bleakness darkened his expression. "You hate me so much that you won't even reveal whether my child is a boy or a girl?"

She didn't answer, and eventually he lifted his shoulders in a small shrug. "It doesn't matter. I shall soon see for myself. Get into the car."

"No, I won't."

"I only suggested it because you're shivering," he said tersely.

"You're all heart," Beth snapped. The first shock of their encounter had passed and she was beginning to think clearly once again. She had devised an emergency escape route as soon as she started working at the supermarket and she knew exactly where she needed to take Luke if she was to increase her chances of evading him. He wouldn't be easy to fool, but she had acquired a lot of useful new skills during the past twenty-seven months, including the ability to act out a wide variety of roles. In the past, pride would have prevented her from showing a helplessness she didn't feel. Nowadays pride took a decided second place to practicality. Beth needed only a split second to realize that she had to lull Luke into a false sense of security. Once she had persuaded him to lower his guard, she could utilize her intimate knowledge of the neighborhood to make good her escape. Knowing Luke, she thought that a subtle pretense of hostility mingled with helpless resignation ought to throw him off the track just long enough to give her the head start she needed.

Somehow, despite her bowstring-tension, she managed to squeeze out a few tears. "I'm not going anywhere with you," she muttered, her voice sullen.

She dashed away the tears, sniffing a couple of times for good measure. "I won't get in the car."

"Beth, don't be ridiculous," he replied quietly. "Your lips are turning blue with cold. I only want you to be warm, for heaven's sake."

She jerked her shoulder out from under his restraining hand and pretended to shrug with impotent fury. Luke's touch made her acutely uncomfortable, and she was glad to avoid his gaze as she got into the car, slamming the door behind her.

He took his seat behind the wheel, and clasping her hands tightly in her lap, she stared down at the white gleam of her knuckles. Her tension, she acknowledged, wasn't entirely because of the part she was playing. Luke's nearness had always had a devastating effect upon her senses.

"You can threaten me all you want," she said, hurriedly forcing herself back into her role. "I won't take you to see my child. I have a legal right to deny you access and I'll never surrender that right."

"You still think like a lawyer, don't you, Beth? But you've forgotten something important. I think like a lawyer, too, and I've been a lawyer eight years longer than you have.''

He reached into the breast pocket of his jacket and pulled out a neatly folded document. "This is a court order," he said softly, "issued by the state of Rhode Island, which is the state with most claim to jurisdiction in our case. This order demands that my child be brought back to Newport for a custody hearing. In the meantime, I'm to be given unlimited access to him. Or her. We can settle this thing amicably, Beth, or I can go and call in a fleet of state troopers. Which one of those options do you want to take?''

The sickness in her stomach swelled ominously, and she clutched her arms across her waist. This time, there was no need for her to feign fear. She was sure he could see it stamped into every line of her face and across every curve of her body. It was the certain knowledge that she could never defeat Luke Caine in a court of law that had kept her running for almost two and a half years. Unless she managed to escape, she knew she would lose her child permanently. And if Uncle Peppe's henchmen had their way, she might be lucky to escape with her life. She wasn't acting at all when she turned to look at Luke, her expression hard and angry with defiance.

"I read in *Newsweek* magazine that you're a hot prospect to contest the next senatorial election in Rhode Island. If you try to win custody of...of our child, I'll go to the media and tell them exactly why I left you. I wonder how much hope you'd have for a senatorial nomination by the time I finished telling them all about you?''

He put the key into the ignition, his dark features suddenly alight with bitter mockery.

"That's certainly an interesting question, Beth. Tell me, which dreadful revelation were you planning to make first? That shrimp in garlic-butter sauce is my favorite food? That I have a secret passion for watching old monster movies on my video recorder? Or maybe you plan to go straight for the heavy stuff. Are you going to tell the media that I have an insatiable sexual appetite? That during the year of our marriage we made love almost every night and sometimes twice on the weekends? What effect would that have on the Senate race, I wonder? Do you think the worthy citizens of Rhode Island approve of sex on Sundays?"

She pushed away the erotic images that his words evoked. Memories could be dangerous, and their mutual passion was not something she cared to remember—ever.

"None of those things," she said quietly. "But I plan to tell them precisely why I was forced to leave you."

She noticed that his hands tightened on the steering wheel, but his voice remained as light as ever.

"Now that should make fascinating reading for a lot of people, but especially for me. Do I have to wait until your revelations hit the newsstands or might I be treated to an advance version? I assume it wasn't the garlic shrimp that dealt the fatal blow, so precisely why did you leave me, Beth? I confess that I've often wondered about that during the past couple of years."

"Don't play games with me, Luke," she said bitterly. "You know why I left you. I'm not a naive idealistic fool anymore. It's tough to find work when you don't want to produce any references, and I've been brushing against the shady side of the law almost every day for the past two years. You learn fast when you work as a hostess in a strip joint, even faster than you do as a junior assistant in a D.A.'s office. My eyes are now permanently open to what's going on around me. Sometimes, these days, I even seem to sleep with my eyes open. I'm no longer an innocent young lawyer fresh out of law school who thinks that everybody sworn into public office wants to serve the public good."

"Uncle Peppe's dead and Aunt Maria says she's going to retire to Florida," he said with seeming irrelevance, but his

words confirmed Beth's suspicion that Luke knew exactly
why she had left Rhode Island so precipitously. "Uncle
Peppe died eighteen months ago," he added.

"Well, I sure hope that the boys gave him a wonderful
funeral," she replied, unable to keep the sarcasm out of her
voice. "Or did he have to make do with the traditional concrete coffin somewhere out in the bay?"

"Uncle Peppe died of cancer," Luke said, backing the car
out of its parking place. "The disease was diagnosed soon
after we married, and he was bedridden for three months
before he died."

"I'm sorry." The two clipped words were the closest she
could come to any conventional expression of sympathy,
and after a moment's silence Luke drove the car toward the
parking lot exit. He paused at the stop sign.

"If I do decide to run for the Senate, Beth, the media
won't need any persuasion from you to rake up everything
they can about my connections to Uncle Peppe, so I'm
afraid that particular threat carries no weight with me. My
aunt married Peppe before I was born and against the wishes
of everybody in her family. But if the voters want to hold me
responsible for her actions, then there's nothing I can do
about it."

There was an angry beep of the horn from the car behind
them, and Luke eased out of the parking lot into the flow of
suburban Saturday traffic. "I need directions for the baby-
sitter's house," he said. "Or directions to wherever it is that
you keep my child while you're at work."

She felt a betraying flush of anticipation rise in her cheeks
and hoped he would misunderstand its cause. If her plan
was to work, she needed to keep Luke driving for ten minutes or so and then bring him back to a street only two
blocks away from the supermarket. His sense of direction
was normally excellent, but she had no other choice than to
try to confuse him. There was no way she could leave Col-

orado without her car, and her car was in the back parking lot at the supermarket. Fortunately Denver's system of one-way streets would work very much to her advantage. She knew this part of town intimately, but Luke had no familiar landmarks to help orient him.

"The sitter lives in Aurora," she said, carefully injecting a note of utter weariness into her voice. "Her apartment building is about ten minutes' drive from the store. You need to turn left at the next traffic signal, then left again. It's a one-way system around here, so I'll tell you when to make the next turn."

He nodded, then glanced into the rearview mirrors and changed lanes. He seemed to have no desire for further conversation, and Beth was grateful for the silence. Her mouth was so dry from nerves that it was hard to speak, and she needed every ounce of her concentration in order to misdirect him successfully.

She gave curt instructions that led him on a ten-block sweep around the supermarket. She took care never to have Luke turn onto a street with a view of the mountains. He almost certainly knew that the Rocky Mountains lay west of Denver, and she didn't want to provide him with any obvious reference point. The streets through which she guided him were entirely featureless, the sort of generic suburban development that defied recognition on only brief acquaintance.

"You have to turn right at the next set of traffic lights," she said when she finally brought him back within a block and a half of the store. She could almost feel the adrenaline surge through her body, and her stomach coiled tight with anticipation. She had to fight to keep her voice level.

"The sitter's apartment is halfway down the block. It's on the ground floor of a colonial-style building off to your right." With any luck, if he looked to the right, he wouldn't see the narrow alleyway opening immediately to his left.

He followed her directions without comment, drawing the Buick to a halt outside the neatly painted entrance of a three-story building.

"Is this the place?" he asked.

"Yes, this is the one."

"Let's go, then." He put the gearshift into park, removed the keys from the ignition and dropped them casually into his right-hand pocket.

The sun still shone with its usual brilliance and the day was quite warm for November, but Beth's body had turned to ice. She fumbled with her seat belt, her fingers apparently so clumsy that she couldn't unfasten the buckle. She was no longer quite sure how much of her nervousness was acting and how much was genuine. The seat belt really did seem to be jammed.

"Luke... I'm sorry... I can't make this catch work...."

"Here, let me. The equipment in these rental cars can sometimes be a problem."

He leaned across the seat, and she slipped her left hand behind his elbow, as if making more space for him to maneuver. His arm grazed her breast, and he muttered an apology as he bent forward, pressing the catch to unfasten the belt. She closed her eyes, scarcely daring to breathe as she slipped her hand into his coat pocket. She heard the click of the seat belt just as her fingers closed around the car keys and she deliberately moved her body so that her breast thrust sharply against his arm. She jerked away, pretending confusion, then smothered a quick sigh of satisfaction when she saw the faint trace of color that flared briefly along his prominent cheekbone.

"I'm sorry," he said, his words clipped. "Did I hurt you?"

"It's okay." She just managed to keep the tremor out of her voice. Trying to feign casualness, she moved the hand holding the precious car keys back against her body. The silence in the car seemed filled with tension, but she couldn't think of anything to say.

"Er, thanks for your help," she murmured.

"You're welcome." Luke spoke curtly. He pushed open his door, blinking in the fierceness of the midday sun. When he saw that she wasn't following him out of the car, he looked at her with unexpected gentleness.

"Stop procrastinating, Beth. I've waited two years to see my child and I don't intend to wait any longer."

"I'm coming," she said, making her voice sullen once again. If she was too compliant, Luke would become suspicious. She climbed out and, while she was still hidden by the car, allowed her purse to slip slowly down the side of her leg to land with a faint thud on the pavement beside the front wheel.

She joined Luke, and together they walked up the shallow stone steps that led to the apartment lobby. Beth kept her hands inside the pockets of her jacket. She was shivering, and yet at the same time she could feel sweat gathering in hot rivulets along her palms. She knew that if she blew this chance at escape, she would have no chance at another.

When they reached the entrance doors to the apartment building, she stopped and placed her hand on his forearm.

"Luke, promise me that you won't do anything to upset . . . our child." She was pleased to hear that nervous anticipation made her voice sound convincingly husky.

For a moment, she could have sworn she detected a flash of real pain in his eyes. "I'm not a monster, Beth, merely a very frustrated parent. Of course I don't plan to make any unnecessary scenes."

"Thank you. He's only a very little boy and he gets scared quite easily."

"A little boy?" Luke's words emerged on a swift sigh. "I have a son?"

She hesitated for a carefully calculated moment. "Yes. His name's Christopher. I thought you ought to know before we go inside. I don't want this meeting to be any more traumatic for him than it needs to be."

"I've given you my word, Beth. After all, he's my son, too. So, how do we get this entrance door open? Do we buzz?"

Now! she thought. Now was the moment when her plans had to work. Thank God that in the old days she had always been a bit scatterbrained about personal possessions, so he probably wouldn't question her ploy for a few vital seconds. And with luck, seconds would be all she needed. She pressed her hands to her hot cheeks, doing her best to look flustered and dithery.

"Oh, Luke, I've left my purse in your car! We need a key for these doors, or we won't be able to get in. Wait here and I'll go grab my purse. You didn't lock the car, did you?"

She gave him no chance to answer, no chance to reflect. She ran down the shallow flight of stairs, her feet moving rapidly in the flat, rubber-soled shoes she always wore for work. She reached the far side of the car and bent down in a single fluid motion to retrieve her purse from the pavement. Then she began to run. With a sudden burst of speed, she tore across the street and into the narrow alley opposite the building where she had left Luke.

The rear entrance to another apartment building backed onto the alley a few feet beyond a slight curve. She heard Luke's bellow of rage just as she dashed inside the building. The entrance was concealed, and there was a chance— if only a slim one—that Luke wouldn't realize where she had gone.

She had no time to be frightened, no time to wonder if he was catching up on her. Every scrap of her energy was concentrated on moving as fast as she could along her predetermined route. She dashed through the lobby of the apartment building and emerged from the front entrance, an entire block away from where she had left Luke.

The suburban branch of a major department store was now facing her, and she sprinted across the parking lot and raced through the store. She whipped past the gloves and the jewelry counter and headed for the men's wear department. Out of the corner of her eye, she saw a nondescript man suddenly start moving toward her and realized that her frantic running had attracted the attention of a store detective.

She certainly had no time to stop and explain. She dodged around a large lady, who conveniently spilled the contents of her numerous shopping bags all over the floor, then headed for the fire exit positioned between men's overcoats and boys' jeans. The heavy steel door bore the sign Emergency Use Only. Her situation, Beth thought with a flash of grim humor, was definitely an emergency. She heaved against the bar with all her strength and emerged into the sunlight of another parking lot. The dry air rasped in her lungs, and her breathing had become excruciatingly painful. She was in excellent physical condition but she had never run this fast in her life before.

She raced across the lot. One more street to cross and she would be at the rear of the supermarket. She ran, listening subconsciously for the wail of a police siren or the pounding of Luke's feet. She heard neither.

She made it to her car more by instinct than by anything else. She slumped against the door as she searched inside her purse for the keys. Her heart pounded so hard that her hands were shaking in unison with her heartbeat. She unlocked the car door, feeling the keys slip in her sweaty hands as she turned on the ignition. The engine responded at the first touch of the key, but she resisted the urge to push down on the accelerator and roar out of the parking lot. With supreme effort, she made herself pause long enough to take several deep calming breaths. Blind panic and driving a car were two activities that didn't go well together.

When her breathing finally returned to something approaching normal, she scrubbed her hands against her slacks to wipe away the sweat and reversed out of the parking space. She edged into the flow of cars leaving the supermarket, taking what seemed slightly longer than a lifetime to reach the highway. She drove for less than two minutes before coming to the intersection of one of Denver's main east-west thoroughfares. She glanced in her rearview mirror. There was still no sign of pursuit.

With a tiny triumphant exclamation, she headed the car east. She felt inside her pocket and touched Luke's car keys, and for a fleeting instant, a grin curved her mouth. She hoped the rental company would take a long time to provide him with a duplicate set. She hoped even more fervently that he would spend several cold and useless hours staking out her apartment, waiting to see his child. Naturally she had no intention of returning to her apartment, which was rented furnished, with each week paid for in advance. Beth learned quickly, and she had soon learned the discipline of traveling light and keeping all essential items packed in her car. Two suitcases of clean clothes were hidden in the trunk, with a carton of canned and packaged groceries nestled between them, and her money—all four hundred and sixty-nine dollars of it—was in an envelope stuffed deep inside the lining of her purse.

After half an hour of careful circling, Beth felt confident nobody was on her tail, but she took another quick sweep around the area before heading west out of Aurora. She drove steadily, the car radio tuned to an all-news station. Snow was threatened to the north but not to the south, which made the decision to drive south into New Mexico an easy one. The only disadvantage of such a route was the scarcity of population and the chance that gas station attendants or motel owners might remember her. But Santa Fe wasn't too far away and it was a large enough city to lose herself in easily. It was a myth, she had found, that giant metropolitan areas were the only safe places to go underground.

The mountains loomed ahead of her, silhouetted against the cloudless winter brilliance of the sky, but she scarcely noticed them. She turned right onto Colorado Boulevard, heading toward the downtown area of Denver. Gradually her tense muscles began to relax. The streets behind her were clear. Nobody was in pursuit. It was time to go to the babysitter's house.

It was time to go and pick up Kristin.

CHAPTER TWO

THE ELDERLY WOMAN peered through the narrow opening of the door, her face creasing into a smile of welcome as soon as she saw Beth.

"Well, hello, luvvy," she said, taking off the chain and flinging the door wide. "Fancy seeing you at this hour of the day. Come on in."

"Hi, Jessie." Beth followed the sway of the sitter's plump purple-clad hips down the hallway. Jessie Bryant was a retired actress with a distinct taste for the dramatic, but Beth had quickly realized that her exotic exterior and abrupt speech masked a genuine love of small children and a heart that was slightly softer than butter.

She waited while the sitter unlatched the child-proof gate that guarded the entrance to her living room. A little girl sat in front of the mock fireplace, intent upon stacking a selection of empty margarine containers into a tall and somewhat wobbly pyramid.

"Kristin, honey, there's somebody here to see you," Jessie said, and the toddler looked up. She had dark blue eyes set in a round, pink-cheeked face, and a mop of mousy brown curls. Her body was still chubby with the plumpness of babyhood, but her long legs suggested that one day she would be tall and slender like her mother. Her entire face lit up when she saw Beth. She lurched to her feet, grasping a yellow plastic bowl, and her mouth widened into an ecstatic smile. She trotted across the room at lightning speed, her curls bobbing as she walked.

"Mama!" she exclaimed, hugging Beth's knees. "Hi Mama! Me is here! Bye-bye Jessie. Me go home now."

"Hello, honeybun. How are you doing?" Beth smiled as she ruffled Kristin's soft brown hair. She fought the irrational urge to grab her daughter and run blindly from Jessie's house. Logically she knew that there wasn't any immediate need for haste, but her nervous system was working in a more primitive rhythm than her intellect, and she couldn't shake the conviction that every second counted.

She gave her daughter's hand a comforting squeeze, not quite sure whether she was reassuring herself or her child.

"Go and fetch your jacket, Kristin, please. We're leaving now and we're in a bit of a hurry."

Kristin obediently trotted to the far side of the room and removed a bright blue quilted jacket from the corner armchair. She carried the jacket back to Beth, looking extremely pleased with herself.

"Mine," she announced, clutching it to her stomach. "We go home now." She didn't wait for an answer but ran toward the door.

Jessie chuckled and scooped the child up as she flashed past.

"Whoa, there, little one. I have to talk to your Mama for a minute or two." She turned to Beth.

"Did you get off work early, luvvy? That's unusual for a Saturday, isn't it?"

"Yes, it is, but there were special circumstances. I asked the manager for a favor...." Beth's voice trailed off into a calculated vagueness. She hated to lie to a woman who had shown her and Kristin nothing but kindness, but she had learned that it was often necessary to deceive good people. For Jessie's own sake, it was best if she knew as little as possible about Beth's past and absolutely nothing about Beth's plans for the future.

"We've had an unexpected invitation to spend a week in the mountains," she said, lifting Kristin out of the sitter's arms and into her own. "Steve, this friend of mine, owns a condominium in Vail and he's asked me to go skiing with him. The store agreed to give me a week's unpaid leave." She grimaced as she elaborated on her lie.

"I can't afford the time off really, but the chance for a week's skiing is too good to miss. My friend is divorced and he has a little girl of his own, so Kristin can stay with her in the nursery. It'll make a pleasant change for both of us."

"It certainly will." Jessie beamed her pleasure. She was a true romantic and was delighted to think that her favorite client planned a vacation with her boyfriend. A divorced man with young children was usually a prime candidate for matrimony, and in Jessie's considered opinion, Beth needed a husband even more than Kristin needed a father.

"You work too many hours each week, luvvy, and you deserve a chance to enjoy yourself. Come to think of it, you're looking a bit harassed today. Those luscious blond curls of yours aren't quite as bouncy as usual."

"Maybe I need one of those revitalizing shampoos they're always advertising on television." Beth forced another casual smile, though her face felt as if it were cracking.

"Anyway, Jessie, I have to get out of here and start my packing. Steve wants us to get on the road before snow shuts down the passes. Could I have Kristin's bag, please?"

"Of course, my dear." The sitter opened the hall closet and retrieved a large nylon duffel bag. "Here it is. Kristin's blanket and toys and her special Garfield mug are all in there." Jessie's smile was teasing as they walked together to the front door.

"You cram so much into this bag, Beth, I shouldn't think you need to pack anything extra for your week in the mountains. It's all in here already!"

"Our apartment's small and I've found that it's easier to keep everything Kristin needs in one place." Beth's voice sounded nonchalant. "But you're right, Jessie! A couple of sweaters and some pajamas, and Kristin's packing will be complete."

She didn't explain the real reason for the full bag. Beth had been forced to abandon Kristin's teddy bear in Nebraska when she had spotted two detectives waiting outside the door of their apartment. She had driven into Kansas with her daughter's pitiful sobs ringing nonstop in her ears. Every cry had torn at her heart. Since then she had never left the apartment without taking Kristin's favorite blanket and other personal possessions. The precaution had already proven its value. It had paid off when they left Kansas and it was going to pay off again here.

Beth settled her debt with Jessie and said goodbye as quickly as possible while Kristin squirmed excitedly in her arms. Beth had said nothing that her daughter understood, but she sensed something unusual in her mother's attitude.

"Bye-bye, Jessie," Kristin said, giving the sitter an enthusiastic kiss. "Me go home now."

"Goodbye, honey. You have a good time up in the mountains." Jessie returned Kristin's hug affectionately. "Build a big snowman for me, and I'll see you next week."

"We'll do that," Beth said lightly. "Take care, Jessie."

She hurried down the path, smothering her feeling of guilt. When she didn't turn up the following week, Jessie would certainly start to worry. Beth nibbled her lower lip, trying to think of some way to ease the sitter's mind without revealing anything at all about her real plans. She would call at the end of next week, she decided, pretending the call was from Vail. She would claim that Steve, her nonexistent boyfriend, had offered to marry her. Jessie loved weddings and would be too happy to question the story.

Sooner or later, of course, Luke and his detectives would track the sitter down, but Beth had been very careful to hide her secrets and Jessie would have little useful information to pass on. Except for one crucial fact. Jessie would tell Luke that his child was a daughter. A little girl with brown curly hair and huge blue eyes.

Beth hooked the duffel bag over the same arm that held Kristin, and freed a hand to open the creaky iron gate at the entrance to Jessie's small town house. There was nothing she could do to prevent Luke discovering that his child was a girl and nothing she could do to prevent his learning what Kristin looked like, so her only sensible course of action was to forget about the problem. She had trained herself not to worry about things that couldn't be changed. If she had wasted time worrying about the unavoidable during the past two years, she would never have kept herself and Kristin successfully hidden. Optimism suddenly lightened her step. She had managed to hide from Uncle Peppe's minions so far, and there was no reason she wouldn't succeed in the future.

She balanced Kristin awkwardly on her hip as she re-latched the gate. A man stepped out from behind the scraggy overhang of a large evergreen and gripped her tightly around the waist.

"Hello, Beth," he said softly. "Please don't scream or try to run. Neither of us wants to frighten the child."

Beth's arms clenched so convulsively around her daughter that Kristin yelped in protest. "Ouch, Mama! Hurt my tummy!"

"I'm sorry, honeybun, I didn't mean to hurt you." Beth dropped a light kiss on her daughter's cheek, but it was a reflexive action, one that she was scarcely aware of making. Her body felt hollow—weightless at the center but iron-heavy at the extremities. With some distant part of her brain, she realized that what she was experiencing was acute panic mingled with more than a touch of despair, but she was so numb with shock that it was hard to define exactly what she was feeling. Her head felt thick and swollen as she lifted it to look at Luke, and her tongue was suddenly too big to fit inside her mouth.

"How did you find me?" she asked dully.

"This isn't an appropriate place for explanations. Please get into the car, Beth."

He held her tightly beneath the elbow, and her feet followed him obediently toward the royal blue Pontiac parked at the curb. No maroon Buick, she noted stupidly, because of course she had the keys to that. Her feet thumped down on the pavement, one after the other, but her stomach and head felt as if they were floating along separately, somewhere behind and above the rest of her body. She tried to think, but nothing coherent would form inside the black hollow of her mind.

Kristin spoke abruptly into the silence. "Hello, Man," she said.

There was an infinitesimal pause before Luke replied. "Hello, little one. It sure is good to meet you at last. How are you doing?"

Kristin looked at him speculatively. "Me is hungry," she announced.

"Haven't you eaten lunch? It's quite late already. Didn't the sitter give you enough to eat?"

"Me is hungry," Kristin repeated. If she understood the precise meaning of his questions, she clearly considered them irrelevant.

"You can have something good to eat as soon as we get back to your mommy's apartment." There was another brief moment of hesitation. "What's your name, sweetheart?"

"Me is me." Kristin wriggled in her mother's arms. She was obviously bored by the conversation now that the immediate prospect of an ice-cream cone or similar goody had disappeared. She waved her hand. "Bye-bye, Man. Me go home now."

Luke opened the passenger door of the Pontiac. Vaguely Beth registered that he was smiling. "I'm coming with you to your apartment," he said to Kristin. "I want to have a chance to play with you for a while."

The little girl looked less than thrilled at this suggestion. "Mama, play," she said hesitantly, glancing toward her mother. "Me play wiv Mama."

Beth swallowed hard. There still didn't seem to be room inside her mouth for her tongue. "We'll play after lunch," she said thickly. She cleared her throat. "We'll make a snowman if you like."

The words bounced around inside the dark tunnel of her mind, and she wasn't altogether sure they made sense—especially when she remembered that there had been no snow in Denver so far that year.

But Luke didn't give her the opportunity to say anything more. "Get in the car, Beth, and don't try anything fancy. And let me warn you. This time I plan to grab first and ask for explanations afterward, so if you behave sensibly, it will be much more comfortable for all three of us."

His warning was totally unnecessary. Even if she hadn't been holding a twenty-eight-pound toddler and a large duffel bag, she wouldn't have had a hope of escaping him. Her legs were wobbling like pieces of limp pasta, and her eyes weren't seeing clearly. She eased herself into the passenger seat, automatically helping Kristin to settle onto her lap. She was vaguely aware of Luke setting the car into motion and the flow of other cars along the highway, but she was still almost numb when the car drew to a halt in front of her apartment building. She wondered in an unfocused fashion how he had known which direction to take.

"Give me your purse," Luke ordered. "This time I'll find the necessary keys myself."

Meekly she handed over her purse. She didn't move until he spoke again. "Come on, Beth. We have a lot to discuss and it'll be easier inside."

She got out of the car and walked docilely toward the apartment entrance. Four concrete steps led up to the doorway, and she stumbled as she stepped onto the first of them. Luke grabbed her around the waist.

"Here, let me carry the child."

"No, you can't hold her!" She heard the hysteria in her voice and quieted her tone with considerable difficulty. "I'm sorry, but she doesn't respond well to strangers."

Even through her numbness, she was aware that she had said the wrong thing. "Dammit!" Luke exploded. "I'm not a stranger. I'm her father, for God's sake!"

"Biological facts aren't very interesting to a two-year-old. As far as she's concerned, you're a stranger."

"And whose fault is that?" he asked, the bitterness sharp in his voice.

"Yours! It's all your fault! Your... activities made it impossible for me to live with you!"

Kristin, alarmed by their anger, buried her face in Beth's neck. "Man go away," she said, the beginning of a sob catching her words.

Beth stroked her hair. "Hush, honey, it's all right. Mama's here and I won't let you go."

Luke visibly bit back the angry retort that hovered on his lips, and they climbed the stairs in a silence broken only by the clatter of their shoes on the bare wooden steps. He unlocked Beth's apartment door, then held it open so that she could carry Kristin inside. The front door led straight into the tiny living room and she sat on the battered tweed sofa, unzipping Kristin's jacket and refusing to speculate on what Luke must think about her poverty-stricken surroundings. There was new beige carpeting on the floor, but no draperies on the windows and no furniture other than the sofa and a large Formica coffee table. Two children's picture books and a red plastic train provided the only splashes of color in the entire room. The apartment was rented furnished, and Beth had learned three or four moves ago not to waste money on vases or pictures or knickknacks that were all too likely to be abandoned.

As soon as she was free of her jacket, Kristin jumped off her mother's lap and ran for the kitchen. Contrary to what Beth had told Luke, Kristin was normally an exceptionally outgoing child, but for some reason, she seemed to be annoyed with Luke and pointedly ignored him. She circled him carefully as she crossed the tiny hallway.

"Me is hungry, Mama," she said, pausing at the kitchen door.

Luke followed her into the kitchen. "We're all hungry," he said. "What would you like us to eat?"

Kristin scowled up at him, then ran back to her mother's side. She clung like a limpet to Beth's knees. "Mama?" she queried uncertainly.

"I'm right here, honey." Beth swung her daughter into her arms. The familiar press of Kristin's chubby legs made a welcome patch of warmth against her ice-cold body. She still felt incapable of rational thought, but at least her physical reactions now seemed slightly more normal. She could speak without wondering if her words would come out backward.

"Now let me think," she said, gently tickling Kristin's tummy. "What shall I make for you to eat? Would you like a boiled egg?"

"A negg." Kristin's entire body wriggled with approval. "Wiv toast?"

"With toast," Beth agreed. As her daughter had done, she walked past Luke without acknowledging his presence. She sat Kristin on the counter, well away from the stove, and put two slices of bread into the toaster. There were four eggs left in the refrigerator, and she took them all out and placed them in a pan of water. Luke's eyes seemed to be boring a hole in the back of her neck, but she refused to turn around and look at him.

His voice broke into the tense silence. "Would you be good enough to tell me my daughter's name? Unless you're a lot more kinky than you used to be, I assume it isn't Christopher."

The toast popped up and Beth replaced it with another two slices of bread before she replied. "Her name is Kristin."

"Kristin Caine?"

She felt the hot color rise up and stain her cheeks. "No. Kristin Faulkner. She's registered under my maiden name on her birth certificate."

"I suppose it's too much to hope that you filled in my name as the father?"

Beth busied herself with spreading margarine on the toast. "Er, no. If you must know, I left the space for her father's name blank."

"I see. Well, fortunately, that's one document that should be easy to change."

She smiled bitterly. "Personally I like it just the way it is."

"If you think my daughter is going through life with a blank on her birth certificate where it asks for the name of her father, then you can think again. I want you to give me her exact date of birth and the name of the county and state where she was born, and I'll see that my lawyers make the necessary alterations as soon as we're back in Newport."

She whirled around to face him. "What makes you so all-fired certain that I'm coming back to Rhode Island? You can't keep me tied to your side with a ball and chain, you know."

He looked at her coolly. "It's your choice, of course. As you point out, I can hardly carry you handcuffed onto the plane. But make no mistake about it, Beth, I'm leaving here at eight o'clock tomorrow morning and Kristin is coming with me. I imagine the experience will be rather traumatic for her if she has to make the journey alone.''

"You're a bastard, Luke," she whispered. "Did I ever remember to tell you that?"

His features became taut. "I don't think so, but then, in-depth communication doesn't seem to have been the strong point of our marriage. As I recall, the last time we were together we spent a stimulating couple of hours going wild in my bed. Your remarks on that occasion weren't altogether coherent, but from what I managed to hear between sighs and moans, you certainly called me several interesting names. If I remember correctly, however, bastard wasn't one of them."

Beth closed her eyes, shutting out the vivid, enticing pictures his words had evoked.

"Maybe your memory isn't as good as you think it is," she said bleakly.

He turned away with a brief harsh exclamation, and she returned her attention to the stove. Her hands shook as she extracted one of the eggs from the boiling water and scooped it into a bright red eggcup. She carried the egg and a plate of lightly buttered toast to the kitchen table. She lifted Kristin onto a chair already padded by a thick cushion, then tucked the chair securely against the table. She opened a drawer and removed a red plastic spoon. That left three spoons, two forks and two knives inside the drawer, more evidence that Beth had learned to travel light.

"My spoon!" Kristin exclaimed, grasping the utensil with evident pleasure. She banged experimentally on the table a few times, then began to eat the boiled egg with surprising neatness. She smiled happily at Beth as she crunched on a piece of toast. "My negg!" she added.

"Your egg," Beth confirmed. She rumpled her daughter's curls before turning to confront Luke.

"I'll have to make us egg salad sandwiches," she said stiffly. "I'm sorry, but I don't have any more eggcups."

"That's fine," he replied impatiently. "Tell me, Beth, what exactly was your excuse for running out of the house without telling me where you were going? Did it never occur to you that the people left behind might be worried?"

She clasped her arms around her waist. "Yes, but there was nothing I could do about the situation. I had no choice."

"I suppose you wouldn't like to elaborate just a little on that statement? Or was the note stuck on the refrigerator door supposed to explain it all? 'Luke, I'm sorry, I can't live with you anymore. Beth.' That sure was a nice succinct way to sum up more than a year of marriage. I know I always admired your economy with words, but don't you think that was carrying conciseness a bit too far?"

"For the last three months of our marriage I hardly ever saw you! If you'd ever been home, maybe you'd have been more aware of the problems we were having!"

"What problems?" he asked, his voice dangerously quiet. "The fact that I wanted to make love to you every time I saw you? Or the fact that you went up in flames every time I took you into my arms? Was that the problem I'd have been more aware of if I'd been home more often?"

Beth stuffed her hands into the pockets of her slacks. She could feel them shaking through the cotton lining. "There's more to a marriage than making love, Luke. I was nearly six month's pregnant when I left you. I needed a home where I could bring up my child to share my values. Once I knew what you . . . what Uncle Peppe was really up to . . ."

"Dammit, Beth, Peppe wasn't my blood brother! He was an uncle by marriage! For Aunt Maria's sake, I saw him maybe four times a year. What the hell did his activities, legal or otherwise, have to do with our marriage?"

She avoided meeting his eyes. "Uncle Peppe wasn't the only problem, even though we both know his activities were strictly illegal...."

"Okay, so Uncle Peppe was a corrupt lawyer. He laundered money for clients you and I wouldn't have touched in a thousand years. He defended clients he knew were guilty of rotten crimes. I guess we both know that there were a couple of judges he paid off on a regular basis. He had lawyers working in his office who should have been tightly locked up behind prison bars. But dammit, Beth, you weren't married to Uncle Peppe! You were married to *me*."

"I told you. It wasn't only Uncle Peppe—"

"Then what else was bothering you? Did it never occur to you that it might have been smart to discuss the problems you thought we were having? As far as I knew, everything about our relationship was fine. You were pregnant with our first child and you knew I was looking forward to becoming a father. I was halfway through my third congressional term, and you were thrilled about your recent promotion at the D.A.'s office. That was July the sixteenth. On July the seventeenth, nothing was left of our marriage except a note stuck to the refrigerator door."

"Luke, you must know what happened. Please don't pretend ignorance. Not now. Not anymore."

"Like hell I know what happened! I wasn't even at home the week you left Rhode Island. I was in Washington, D.C. when the housekeeper called to tell me about your note. What in heaven's name could have been so urgent that you had to leave our house without even stopping to explain why or where you were going?"

Without their realizing it, Beth's and Luke's voices had been rising as they spoke, and Kristin stopped eating. She reached out toward her mother, instinctively seeking reassurance, then glared at Luke, rejection frozen into every rigid line of her body.

"Go home, Man," she said. "Bye-bye, Man."

If anything, the tension in the small kitchen increased, but the anger in Luke's hard features vanished completely as he squatted beside his daughter's chair.

"Kristin, I'm not going away, not right now. I'm going to spend the night in your house. I'm your fa—" He bit off the word and paused a moment before continuing. "Honey, I would like very much to be your friend. Do you think we could be friends?"

Kristin's lower lip thrust out aggressively, and two fat tears trickled down her cheeks. "My Mama," she said. "My house. Man is bad. Man go away *now*."

Luke thrust his hand through his hair and swore quietly beneath his breath. Beth cuddled her daughter consolingly, unable to repress a brief selfish flare of satisfaction. It was reassuring to know there were some things even the Caine family fortune couldn't buy.

Abruptly Luke rose to his feet. "I'll leave you to eat your lunch," he said to Beth. "I don't feel too hungry right at the moment, and there are several things I should do. For a start, I have to arrange for somebody to pick up your car and drive it here to the apartment. I assume it has most of your important luggage in the trunk?"

She avoided his gaze. "Yes. Almost everything we need."

"There are a great many questions I want to ask you, Beth, and you can't always avoid answering me. You won't be able to hide behind Kristin forever. Does she take an afternoon nap?"

Beth hesitated. "Yes, usually," she said at last.

"Good. We'll talk when she's in bed. Is your phone in the living room?"

"Yes, it is."

Kristin curled her arms around Beth's neck and looked defiantly at Luke over her mother's shoulder. "Bye-bye, Man," she said.

There was more than a touch of weariness in Luke's grim smile. "You and Kristin certainly seem to share an unflattering opinion of me," he said to Beth. "But since I'm already heartily sick of being called Man, do you think if you worked on it for a while you could teach my daughter to call me Daddy?"

Kristin gave Beth no chance to reply. She stared at Luke balefully. "Go away, Man," she said. "Go home now."

CHAPTER THREE

BETH SETTLED KRISTIN for her afternoon nap, acutely aware of Luke's silent presence in the bedroom doorway. She had tried to follow her daughter's usual nap-time routine, but she wasn't succeeding very well. Kristin normally bounced around on her bed, demanding stories and songs before she would lie down. Today she snuggled meekly under the covers, clutching her faded baby blanket and clasping her arms around her mother's neck in a fierce hug.

"Mama stay," she whispered, her glance sliding away from Luke's deceptively indolent figure.

"Of course I'll stay," Beth said, trying her best to sound calm and friendly. "Look, Teddy's already asleep."

She put a fat yellow bear with mournful brown eyes on her daughter's pillow, and Kristin looked at the toy consideringly. It was a replacement for the bear left behind in Nebraska, and she had never quite accepted the substitution. "Teddy's not asleep," she said finally.

"I'll pat his tummy," Beth replied. "That should help him to fall asleep. He likes it when I pat his tummy."

"Teddy doesn't like Man."

"Doesn't he?" Beth took care not to turn her gaze toward the doorway. "But the, um, man likes Teddy, and he wants Teddy to take a nap so that he'll grow big and strong."

"Teddy's big and strong now," Kristin said, wriggling around beneath the covers.

"Sure he is. But he'll be even stronger after a nap." Beth ran her fingers gently through her daughter's hair, and after a few minutes, Kristin's wriggles ceased. Beth moved her hand lower and stroked Kristin's back in a slow soothing rhythm. With her other hand she gave an occasional pat to the bear's protruding yellow stomach.

"Mama stay," Kristin murmured sleepily.

"I'm going to be here, honeybun, don't worry. I'll be here all the time you're asleep."

Kristin's convulsive grasp on her blanket gradually loosened. She gave one last angry look toward the doorway, then stretched out her hand toward the bear as her eyelids drooped shut. She gave a little snuffle of relaxation, her body twitched, and she was asleep.

Beth tucked the covers around her daughter's shoulders, feeling herself stiffen when she realized Luke had left his position by the door and was now standing at the foot of the bed. He looked down at the sleeping child, his eyes veiled and his expression unreadable.

"She's very beautiful," he said at last, an odd catch in his voice. "Her eyes are exactly the same shade of blue as yours."

"Actually, she looks more like your mother than anybody else," Beth said, then turned away abruptly, startled by her own words. She had never before consciously acknowledged the likeness between her daughter and Luke's mother. Heaven knew, she thought wryly, her mother-in-law wouldn't be flattered by the comparison. Ruth Caine had never made any secret of the fact that she heartily disliked having the daughter of a Kentucky coal miner as her only son's wife, and she had greeted the news of Beth's pregnancy with glacial coldness. As far as Luke's mother was concerned, the Caine family genes had been purified by centuries of inherited wealth and selective breeding. Between them, she and Luke could claim kinship with virtually every New England family of wealth, power or commercial importance. In Mrs. Caine's opinion, Beth's working-class genes, unsanctified by any hint of money, had absolutely no place grafting themselves onto the Caine's aristocratic family tree.

Beth dropped a light kiss on Kristin's cheek and walked out of the bedroom, still not looking at Luke. She had grown up in the past twenty-seven months, and there were days when the memory of her mother-in-law's snobbishness could actually make her smile. Certainly, Beth was no longer haunted by her old fears of unworthiness; she had far more important things to worry about.

She deliberately made no effort to see whether Luke followed her into the living room. She realized that ever since their encounter outside the supermarket that morning, she had been reacting almost reflexively to his actions. If she was ever to formulate a sensible plan of escape, it was past time to stop reacting. She had to take firm control of herself and the situation she found herself in.

The doorbell buzzed just as she was deciding to go into the kitchen and make herself some tea. She went quickly to the front door.

"Who is it?" she asked.

"It's Bill Decker, Mrs. Caine. Luke asked me to stop by and pick up your car keys so that I can fetch your car from the baby-sitter's house."

"Bill Decker," she said, her voice thick with irony. "Of course! How could I have forgotten about you?"

She was tempted to walk away and leave him standing outside the front door, but she realized that such a childish action would achieve little in the way of practical results. She drew back the bolt and swung open the door.

Bill Decker nodded to her politely, his appearance as neat and nondescript as she remembered. "Hello, Mrs. Caine. It's good to see you again."

He stepped into the apartment, and astonishment gleamed momentarily in his eyes as he glanced around the shabby interior of the living room. It certainly was a striking contrast to the living quarters of Luke's family mansion in Rhode Island, Beth thought dryly.

She watched as Bill Decker smoothed his hair over the beginnings of a bald spot and carefully schooled his features into an expression of polite neutrality.

"It's been a long time, Mrs. Caine. How have you been keeping?"

"Just peachy-dreamy, Mr. Decker. How about you?"

Luke emerged at that moment from the bedroom, and Beth crossed to the battered tweed sofa, taking care not to look at either of the men. Once Bill Decker took possession of her car, she knew she'd have no chance of escape. Thinking realistically, she accepted that, if she wanted to stay with Kristin, she would have to fly back to Rhode Island the next day with Luke. The knowledge filled her with despair, but there was no way she would let either of the men see the true state of her feelings.

"Here are my keys," she said coolly, handing them to Bill Decker. "Do you know where the car is parked?"

"Yes, thank you, Mrs. Caine. It's a brown Chevy, parked on Sherston, about two blocks south of Alameda."

"Very good," she said, unable to conceal a sudden flash of bitterness. "I see you've added amateur detective to all your other invaluable roles."

"Bill followed us this morning at my request. He'd rented the Pontiac," Luke said quietly. "That's how I was able to catch up with you so quickly when you ran away."

"Of course," she said. "I should have realized you wouldn't fly out to Denver on your own. After all, you never did move anywhere without one of your loyal henchmen in tow."

Luke's eyes flashed ominously, but Bill intervened before his employer could say anything. "I'll go pick up the car right away, Mrs. Caine. If it's all right with you, I'll transfer your cases straight into the trunk of the Buick—I got a duplicate set of keys for it and drove it here—and then everything'll be ready for the drive to the airport tomorrow morning. I won't need to disturb you again this afternoon."

Beth shoved her hands deep into the pockets of her slacks. "That sounds very efficient," she said tautly. "Don't let me keep you, Mr. Decker."

Luke scarcely waited for the front door to close, before rounding on her. "In future, Beth, I'd be grateful if you'd direct your insults toward me, not toward people who can't defend themselves. Bill Decker isn't my henchman. He's simply a loyal, hard-working employee."

"I know," she said, smiling with false sweetness. "And the Watergate burglars were just loyal servants of the state, following orders. Isn't it sad they all ended up in jail?"

He drew in a sharp impatient breath. "Your comparison is absurd, Beth, and you must know it. Bill Decker has been helping me trace my child, who was illegally removed from my custody. By you, I might add. Unlike the Watergate burglars, Bill hasn't done anything even marginally immoral, let alone illegal."

Maybe not this time, she thought. *But Decker was with you that night in July. I saw him.*

She sank onto the sofa, suddenly aware that she was hovering on the edge of total exhaustion. More to the point, she was behaving irrationally. If she was to escape from Luke again, she needed to lull his suspicions, not exacerbate him by snide remarks and cutting references. At this moment, what she needed most was to find out how he had traced her. Once she knew how she had slipped up, she could do a better job next time of covering her tracks.

"I was thinking of making myself some tea," she said, feigning a casualness she was far from feeling. "Would you like some?"

Luke looked at her assessingly, as if judging the reasons for her sudden change of conversation, and Beth returned his look with all the blandness she could muster.

"A cup of tea sounds terrific," he said finally.

"Come into the kitchen while I make it," she suggested.

He sat down at the rickety kitchen table and watched as she put the kettle on to boil. She reached into the cupboard for two mugs and dropped a tea bag into each.

"I'm sorry," she said tightly, feeling angry with herself because his gaze made her inexplicably nervous. "I don't have a teapot. I had one once, but it got left behind in Pennsylvania."

His mouth twisted, almost as if he found her revelation painful. "That's okay. You know I never was a connoisseur of tea or coffee."

"Ugh, I sure do remember! If it had steam coming out of the cup, you'd drink it."

A tiny grin lightened his expression. "I always used to tell the staffers to make a fresh pot when you came to visit."

"I appreciated the honor!" She couldn't hide the huskiness in her voice as she recalled all the times she'd teased him about his habit of drinking coffee that had turned black and oily after hours of perking, or tea that had been left brewing half the day. When caught up in his congressional work, Luke resembled a coiled spring waiting to be unleashed, and his single-minded concentration left no room for trivialities like freshly brewed coffee. His burning energy and intense dedication had been two of the characteristics that had first attracted her to him.

There was an unexpected intimacy in the shared memory, and she pulled the stopper from the spout of the boiling kettle with shaking fingers. For heaven's sake, what was the matter with her? She surely wasn't going to wax sentimental over Luke's disgusting taste in hot drinks!

"I called Wayne while you were giving Kristin her lunch," Luke said abruptly. "He very much wants to hear from you."

Boiling water splashed onto the counter at the mention of her oldest brother's name. Luke was at her side in a moment. "Have you burned yourself?"

"No, it's all right."

"Let me see." He took her hands without waiting for her permission and inspected them briefly. His touch was completely impersonal, but a faint shiver of awareness made her fingers quiver within his clasp.

He dropped her hands, his face wearing the expressionless mask that now seemed second nature to him. "There doesn't seem to be any damage," he said, reaching for a paper towel and wiping up the spilled water.

She clasped her arms tightly around her waist. "How...how is Wayne?" she asked. "And the family?"

"They're fine. All the better for knowing that you're alive and well and the mother of a healthy baby girl. These past two years have been tough on your family."

She fought against the immediate wave of guilt that swept through her. She hadn't told her parents about Kristin for the simple reason that they would immediately have passed on the information to Luke. "I did call Wayne once after Kristin was born," she said defensively.

"I know. You told him that the baby had arrived and that you were both doing fine. If that was supposed to be the phone call that set your family's mind to rest, let me tell you that it didn't succeed. Hell, Beth, you didn't even say whether your baby was a boy or a girl. You didn't say where you were calling from. In two years, you never contacted your own father or mother except for a call at Christmas, and even then you hung up as soon as they asked where you were calling from. What in the name of God had they ever done to offend you?"

"Nothing!" she cried out. "But I couldn't tell them anything because I knew they'd pass whatever I said on to you. You know what my family is like. They think that a woman's place is always with her husband, whatever the circumstances."

"You know, there's a lot of people out there who have the same idea," Luke said softly. "I kind of think a wife's place is with her husband, too. At least until she's given him some chance to work out their problems."

Beth lifted the tea bags out of the mugs. She'd let them brew far too long, and the tea was a murky shade of brown. "Here," she said shakily. "I assume you still take it without milk or sugar?"

"Yes. Any old way is fine." He took a sip. "Well, since you won't talk about our marriage, let's talk about our child. I'm Kristin's father, Beth, and I have a right to some basic information. Where was she born? And when is her birthday? How much did she weigh? When did she start walking?"

Beth swallowed hard. "She was born on September third in Philadelphia in the city hospital. She weighed seven pounds fourteen ounces and she started walking two days after her first birthday."

"Any special reason why you chose Philadelphia?" he asked quietly.

"None, except that it's a big enough city to lose myself in."

He pushed his empty mug away and stood up, unconsciously kneading the taut muscles at the back of his neck. It was a gesture she knew well, one of the few signs of fatigue he ever permitted himself, and she closed her eyes momentarily, shutting out the aching familiarity of the sight.

"I didn't think to look in Philadelphia right away," Luke murmured. "When I first read your farewell note, I assumed you'd gone back to Kentucky. I couldn't find any trace of you there, of course, so I started searching in Virginia. Since you'd been to law school there, it seemed a logical place to look. Then we tried Washington D.C. in case you'd gone back to the public defender's office. It took me at least six months to realize that you were deliberately avoiding any place where you'd ever lived before, and that you weren't attempting to practice as a lawyer."

Beth thought briefly of her jobs as gas station cashier, cocktail waitress, bartender and short-order cook in various places of dubious respectability. Anywhere, in fact, that would employ her during the evening hours when Kristin was sleeping and it was easier to find sitters. Anywhere that wouldn't inquire too deeply into her make-believe job record and phony references.

"No," she said, smiling grimly. "I haven't been attempting to practice as a lawyer." She drained the last of her tea and rinsed the mug in the sink. She kept her back turned to Luke as she prepared herself to ask the vital question, the one piece of information she really needed to have before she could attempt to hide from him again.

"So how did you find me in the end, Luke?"

She sensed his hesitation before he replied. He had a brilliant analytical mind and he undoubtedly guessed why she was asking the question. It was a measure of his confidence, she thought bleakly, that he answered her after only a split-second delay.

"We traced you through your social security number. Debt collection agencies have perfected a computerized system of checking new employment records. The day before yesterday I was notified that you'd started work in a Safeway supermarket at the end of last August. I hired a

Colorado detective agency to trace your home address and I flew out here with Bill Decker on Friday."

So, she thought tiredly, in the end it had been that simple for him to track her down. A couple of phone calls and twenty-seven months of frantic running were over. She'd known she was taking a risk when she filled out the job application and gave her true social security number, but Kristin was costing more to feed and clothe every day, and Beth had grown tired of being exploited by shady employers who paid below minimum wages in return for asking no awkward questions. It wasn't encouraging to think that if she went on the run again, she faced a future of supporting Kristin on underpaid jobs poised barely on the right side of the law.

"You were lucky to keep Kristin hidden for so long," Luke said, breaking into her uneasy thoughts. "I've had private detectives in every state working on finding her. They almost caught up with you once in Nebraska."

"I know," she said. "But fortunately, I've developed an acute sense of smell. I can sniff out a private detective or a regular policeman at forty paces. I saw those men waiting outside my apartment building and I never went back there."

"Yes, I read their report. Like you, I've discovered that most law-enforcement officials aren't very good at subtle disguises." His voice was little more than a murmur, and yet she had no difficulty in hearing the menace implicit in his words. "That's why, this time, I came for you myself."

"I guess I should be flattered by your prompt personal attention," she said, masking her feelings with a brittle smile. "I certainly never managed to get that sort of treatment while we were married."

He moved toward her with incredible swiftness and, putting an arm on each side of her body, trapped her against the sink. "Is that why you ran away, Beth? Because you thought I was neglecting you?"

His closeness unnerved her, and she nearly snapped out that of course she hadn't run away for such a trivial reason. Common sense returned just in time. Obviously she couldn't tell him the truth—the fact that she couldn't was why she'd run away in the first place. Just as obviously, he was going to demand some explanation of why she had disappeared into the hot darkness of a July night. Oddly enough, it hurt to realize that he thought of her as immature and irresponsible enough to have run away in a fit of childish pique. Practically speaking, however, she knew she ought to encourage him in such a view.

"I didn't leave Rhode Island just because you neglected me," she said. "There were . . . I went because of a combination of reasons."

"Name two," he demanded softly.

"Uncle Peppe," she said, a hint of defiance in her voice. "And your refusal to talk to me."

"Maybe we didn't talk enough," he admitted. "But I don't see how you solved our problem by running away and making it impossible for me ever to talk to you again. Disappearing for two years wasn't a very smart solution, Beth."

She knotted her fingers together in frustration. "Dammit, Luke, you're doing just what you always did! You're making it sound as though I'm moronic and you're the light of sweet reason! God knows, I did try to tell you what was bothering me. Every time you came home from Washington—which wasn't all that often—I'd try to get you alone, away from your mother and your aunt and Uncle Peppe and Bill Decker—or one of your other two-dozen aides and political consultants. But the only time we ever actually seemed to be alone was when we were in bed. And once we were in bed, you sure didn't have any intention of talking! Every time you didn't want to answer one of my questions, you'd start to make love to me."

She dashed her hand across her mouth, subconsciously brushing away images that still had the power to hurt her. "Don't you know what happened to me in the last weeks of our marriage, Luke?" Her voice throbbed with the uncontrollable ache of remembered pain. "Don't you understand that I got to the stage where I hated you kissing me?"

"Why?" he asked, his voice colder than ice. "Because I could always make you respond? Is that what made you so angry?"

"Yes!" she yelled. "Yes, yes, yes! Don't you see that it's wrong to keep using sex to avoid talking to your own wife? Don't you understand that I felt degraded every time you forced my body to respond against my better judgment? For the last two months of our marriage, we weren't two people making love. We were two bodies mating in the dark!"

A strange gleam came and went in the depths of his gray eyes. "That's not completely true," he said coolly. "Whatever you were doing, Beth, I was always making love when we were in bed together."

Sudden insidious heat shot through her. She moved quickly, but he moved even faster, bringing their bodies into an intimate contact she wasn't prepared for. He bent his head until he was so close that she could feel his breath caressing her cheek.

"Can you remember the last time we kissed?" he murmured. "You were six months pregnant, and I put my hand against your stomach—like this. And when your lips touched mine, I felt our baby kick against my palm." He raised his head and looked into her half-closed eyes. "You took my hand and put it—here." He slid his hand slowly up from her stomach to rest against the swell of her breast. "Do you remember, Beth?"

"No," she whispered hoarsely. "I don't remember . . . anything."

"Strange," he said softly. "And I remember it so clearly." His fingers wove a delicate sensual pattern over the curve of her breasts while his thumbs grazed lightly across her nipples. His lips brushed hers, moving softly against her mouth, not angry or demanding, but almost coaxing in their gentleness.

She tried to close her mind to the devastating pleasure of what he was doing, but it wasn't her mind he was touching, and her body, unfortunately, seemed to have a will of its own. Her skin felt hot, strangely sensitive and unmistakably alive. A wave of desire washed over her, and clenching her fists hard, she pushed him away.

"Don't!" she said. "I can't bear it when you touch me."

He moved away, but his cool gray eyes drifted over her body in silent mockery. "I'm sorry," he said, "but when you melt in my arms like that, it's hard to remember that you find my kisses degrading."

A slight noise made them both turn around. Kristin stood in the doorway, clutching her teddy bear and dressed only in her T-shirt. She looked at Beth, totally ignoring Luke's presence, and held the bear out accusingly.

"Teddy wet the bed," she said. "Teddy is bad."

Beth quickly picked up her daughter and gave her a hug. "No, Teddy isn't bad at all," she said. "He's just had an accident. I'm really proud of the way he's learning to use the bathroom. Most of the time, Teddy is very good and so are you."

Kristin scowled, still taking care to avoid looking toward the corner of the room where Luke was standing. "Teddy made my panties wet."

Beth felt her mouth curve into a grin as she patted her daughter's naked bottom. "Well, you've already taken care of that problem, haven't you, Kris? Let's go see if there's some clean underwear in your drawer.''

"Is there a laundry in this building? I'll wash the sheets, if you like.''

Beth halted in midstride. She and Kristin stared at Luke with almost equal astonishment, Beth because she couldn't imagine Luke doing something as mundane as laundering sheets, Kristin presumably because she hadn't expected Luke to speak.

"There are washing machines and dryers in the basement," Beth said uncertainly. "Do you think you'll be able to work them?"

"I expect I'll manage to read the printed instructions," Luke said dryly. "It's wonderful what a college degree can teach you these days.''

Beth flushed. "I'm sorry. I didn't mean to sound ungrateful. Thanks for the offer, Luke. This apartment has only three sets of linen, and we'll need the extra set for you.''

He came with them into the bedroom and stripped the sheets with brisk silent efficiency while Beth concentrated on getting Kristin dressed.

She was in the living room, reading Kristin a story, when Luke returned an hour later with a pile of clean neatly folded bed linen. A tiny pair of pink cotton underwear rested on the top of the pile.

It was impossible to guess what Luke was thinking as he looked at them over the pile of sheets. "Your sheets are all warm and dry now, Kristin," he said. "Would you come and help me put them back on your bed?"

Kristin instinctively shrank deeper into Beth's arms. "Stay wiv Mama," she mumbled.

No definable change occurred in Luke's expression, but Beth felt his frustration as if it were her own. For some reason, Kristin's rejection of her father no longer seemed quite as gratifying as it had earlier in the day. Beth sprang to her feet.

"We'd better help him," she said to her daughter. "Luke's never made a little girl's bed before and he might not do it right."

Kristin followed them into the bedroom with obvious reluctance. She clambered onto the room's only chair and watched in silence as the two adults swiftly remade her bed.

"Are there any special arrangements you need to make in order to leave this apartment tomorrow morning?" Luke asked as they tucked in the last blanket.

Beth plumped up the pillow, avoiding Luke's gaze. "Nothing essential. The owner lives in the ground-floor apartment and he has a message box outside his door. We can drop the keys in there with a note saying that I won't be coming back. I don't owe any rent money, plus he has a month's security deposit."

"What about household goods, things like towels? What about your clothes? Don't you need to do some packing?"

She shrugged. "This apartment is rented furnished, so the kitchen equipment and the towels and bed linens aren't mine to take. Almost all our clothes are packed in my car. Kristin and I each have one clean outfit in the bedroom. That's all."

"You've certainly learned to travel light." He straightened and looked abstractedly at the bare white walls and cheap shabby furniture. "Was it worth it, Beth?" he asked softly. "Was our marriage so bad that this was better?"

At that moment, for the first time in twenty-seven months, she suddenly wasn't sure. If she'd known Uncle Peppe was dead, would she have gone back? She wondered. She thrust the thought out of her mind, horrified by her unexpected weakness. That was why Luke was so dangerous. A few hours in his company and he could make her forget the truth. She hadn't left Rhode Island only because of Uncle Peppe. She'd left because her husband—handsome respected Congressman Luke Caine, defender of the oppressed and shining light of his party—was a crook.

She swung around, lifting her chin proudly. "This was better," she said. "And I warn you now, Luke, I'm going to fight you for custody of Kristin all the way."

An unfamiliar bleakness hardened his eyes. "I didn't expect anything different," he said. Turning away from her, he walked across the room to kneel beside Kristin's chair.

"I thought we might go out for dinner," he said casually, scratching her teddy bear between the ears. "Do you like to eat out? I saw a place just down the street where they serve hamburgers and great big ice creams."

Kristin, who usually considered ice-cream cones synonymous with heaven, remained stubbornly silent.

"We could take Teddy with us," Luke continued persuasively. "He could sit in his own special chair."

Kristin looked uncertainly toward her mother. "Mama?" she said.

Beth forced herself to smile. Much as she wanted to frustrate Luke's plans, she wasn't going to use her daughter to do it. "I'd like to eat dinner out, wouldn't you? I'm hungry and we haven't eaten ice cream for a long time."

Kristin nodded her head happily as she jumped down from the chair and ran into the living room, followed by her parents. She picked up her quilted nylon jacket and tried, with no success at all, to fit her arms into the sleeves. Beth was just about to go and help her when Luke swept Kristin onto his lap and quickly fixed the tangled sleeves. He closed the zipper and pressed his finger lightly against his daughter's nose. Kristin didn't smile, nor did she move away, and the two of them stared at each other in tense assessing silence.

It was Luke who moved first. He stood up, carefully setting Kristin on her feet beside him. He held out his hand but didn't forcibly take hers.

"Your mommy has to get her coat and comb her hair," he said. "Shall we wait for her in my car?"

Kristin still didn't speak but she reached up and put her chubby hand into Luke's strong lean fingers.

Beth heard Luke's breath expel in a long sigh. "Meet you downstairs in two minutes," he said to her as he walked toward the front door.

"All right." Her heart was pounding as she closed the front door behind them. To her dismay, she discovered she was crying by the time she picked up her jacket.

She pulled a tissue from the box in the bathroom and scrubbed fiercely at her damp cheeks. She hadn't cried in more than two years of running and she certainly wasn't about to start crying now.

She grabbed a comb and pulled it through her hair, for once in her life feeling grateful for the mop of golden curls that defied any attempt at sophisticated styling. She moistened her lips with pale pink lip gloss, then searched in her purse until she found her compact and dabbed the pressed powder defiantly over her red nose.

She stared into the little bathroom mirror, satisfied that no trace of tears remained visible. Luke might think he had already won the war, but he would soon find out that they had scarcely started the first battle.

CHAPTER FOUR

FROM BETH'S POINT OF VIEW dinner was not a success, although the restaurant was pleasant, serving simple food in bright well-lit surroundings. Their waitress was a cheerful teenager who obviously liked children, and she greeted Kristin with a sunny smile.

"Here's a cookie for you," she said, tucking a plastic bib beneath Kristin's chin and unwrapping a small graham cracker. "Have you brought your daddy and mommy out for dinner?" Her eyes twinkled with friendly laughter. "Your daddy sure looks hungry!"

Kristin glanced angrily toward Luke. "Not my daddy," she said loudly.

There was a painful silence, which Luke broke by calmly ordering a bowl of chili. Beth hastened to add her order of two plain hamburgers and two glasses of milk, and the waitress scurried away, pleased to escape an awkward situation. Beth wished she could get up and scurry away, too. In fact she was more than a little astonished by her daughter's remarks, since she hadn't realized that Kristin even understood what was meant by the words "father" and "daddy." Her daughter's world, so far, had been peopled almost exclusively by women, and Beth had gratefully avoided difficult explanations that didn't seem necessary. In retrospect she realized that she had been willfully blind to Kristin's inevitable curiosity.

The tense atmosphere didn't improve as the evening wore on, although Kristin's humor lightened considerably as she mashed her way through a scoop of vanilla ice cream sprinkled with chocolate. When they returned to the apartment, Luke removed a briefcase and an overnight travel bag from the trunk of his car and walked purposefully into the living room. He spent the remainder of the evening making notes on a statistic-laden congressional report, his manner suggesting total absorption in the complex charts and columns of figures. By nine o'clock, Beth was no longer able to tolerate the strain of sitting silently at the other end of the sofa, pretending to read.

"It's been a long day," she said, getting to her feet and closing her magazine with a snap. "I'm going to bed, Luke. What time do we have to leave here tomorrow morning?"

He glanced up briefly from his report, not really looking at her. "Seven-thirty should do it."

"I'll shower now. Then you can have the bathroom tomorrow morning." She gritted her teeth with the effort of sounding polite. "Does that sound acceptable?"

"Perfectly." This time he didn't even bother to look up. "I'll set my travel alarm for six-thirty. Would you like me to wake you?"

"Thanks, but Kristin will wake me," Beth said, her expression softening into an involuntary smile. "She's much more reliable than any alarm clock."

His head came up suddenly, his eyes steady and hard as he looked at her. He didn't say a word, and she drew a quick deep breath, feeling her cheeks flush as she turned away.

"I'll get the spare sheets for you," she said hurriedly. "The couch isn't very comfortable but at least it's long. You should get a reasonable night's sleep."

"Don't worry about it." He stood up, tossing his congressional report onto the floor and stretching with a surprising hint of weariness. "I saw which drawer you keep the sheets in. I'll get them myself while you're in the bathroom."

"Well, all right. Good night then, Luke."

"Good night."

She was breathing hard as she locked herself in the small bathroom. She had to fight off the sensation that she had somehow escaped from a situation fraught with the promise of danger—a ridiculous sensation, when she thought back over their polite conversation.

She showered quickly, dried off in less than a minute and pulled on an old T-shirt before emerging from the bathroom. She crept into the darkened bedroom and dived under the covers as if she had finally attained a long-sought sanctuary. She could hear the soft sounds of Kristin's breathing, but there was no sound at all from the living room. She wondered if Luke was still reading his report. Maybe he was lying down. Maybe he was already sleeping. She wondered if he still slept in the nude. A picture of his body—lean, hard and slightly tanned—thrust itself relentlessly into her mind, and equally relentlessly, she thrust it out again.

She rolled over onto her stomach, smothering the unwelcome little pulse of excitement that had invaded her body. For the first time since Luke had accosted her outside the supermarket, she had the time and solitude to think clearly about her situation. Why did she feel so panic-stricken, even though she now knew that Uncle Peppe was dead? She had run away to save her life and the life of her unborn child, but it was Uncle Peppe whom she had seen as a threat to her physical safety, not Luke. She had never believed that Luke would harm her physically. In truth, she had never believed that he would physically abuse any other human being.

Since Uncle Peppe was dead, did that mean she could finally stop running? Could she risk fighting for custody of Kristin through the courts? Beth stirred restlessly, then sat up to shake her pillow, which suddenly seemed hot, lumpy and uncomfortable. It wasn't the prospect of a custody fight that really bothered her. She was virtually certain she could win legal custody of her child if she was willing to tell a court of law precisely why she considered Luke Caine an unfit father. And that was the heart of dilemma, Beth reflected. Even now, she wasn't quite sure she was willing to see Luke go to jail.

She leaned back against the headboard, staring unseeingly at the light of the streetlight filtering through the broken slats of the venetian blind. She wasn't in love with Luke—not now, not any more—but she could vividly recall the first time she'd seen him, and the memory still had the power to make her heart ache with a tiny throb of remembered love. Usually she fought against remembering the past, but tonight the memories were irresistible. She squeezed her eyes tightly shut, pressing her face into the pillow as she let the bittersweet images unravel in her mind.

SHE HAD MET LUKE three and a half years ago in Washington D.C. on a typically hot and humid July day. She had passed her bar exams only a few months earlier and had come to the capital as a junior staff member in the public defender's office. She was twenty-four years old, a young lawyer bursting with equal parts of pride and enthusiasm, eager to help the downtrodden and determined to fight for truth, justice and the American way.

She had been slightly less naive than Superman, Beth reflected, but not much. She soon discovered that the downtrodden were usually too apathetic to be helped and that justice had little to do with the cumbersome workings of the American legal system. It hadn't required many weeks in Washington for her to realize that her law school courses had been heavy on idealism but fatally light on practical realities. She wasn't sure which aspect of the legal system offended her more: the ease with which lawyers for professional criminals plea-bargained their clients out of jail or the regularity with which juvenile offenders from the ghetto got punished for the inadequacies of their education, the indifference of their families and the failure of the social programs designed to protect them.

The day she first encountered Congressman Luke Caine had started out routinely enough. She was pleading a case in court. The air-conditioning—true to form—had broken down, and the temperature in the courtroom had hovered slightly above ninety.

As the judge took his seat on the bench, Beth stood, pushing a damp curl from her forehead. She felt wetter and limper than a used dishrag and could only hope that she looked more professional than she felt. At the order of the court clerk, she sat down again then swiveled around to look at her client, James Smith. He was staring dreamily into space, beads of sweat trickling down his gaunt black cheeks and soaking into the neck band of his T-shirt.

James was a seventeen-year-old street kid who had been captured in the act of smashing the lock on Congressman Luke Caine's apartment door. He had threatened the congressman with a loaded handgun, and when he was searched at the police station, it had been discovered that his pockets were stuffed full of cocaine and marijuana. James, who had no family and no permanent address, was found by the prison doctor to be suffering from malnutrition and tuberculosis. Despite her hectic caseload, Beth had tried to interview him on at least three occasions, but he'd sullenly refused to offer any excuses or explanations for his criminal behavior.

In her few months in Washington, Beth had already met a dozen kids like James Smith, and yet she couldn't help sensing something worth salvaging beneath the young man's sluggish, sometimes vicious exterior. She hated to come into court, pleading a case that she knew she hadn't a hope of winning.

As she had feared, the case proceeded with inevitable swiftness. The arresting officer gave his evidence concisely, Beth's cross-examination revealed no breach of the suspect's rights, and the prosecution then called Congressman Luke Caine to the witness stand.

He was much younger than Beth had expected. She discovered she was holding her breath as he walked confidently to the front of the courtroom and took his place on the stand. He wore a conservative gray suit, white starched shirt and maroon silk tie, but something about the casual athletic grace of his movements suggested that he often stripped off his formal clothes and worked out in something a lot less confining than gray pinstripes. He took the stand and recounted his story with the easy clarity of somebody who is well accustomed to speaking in front of an audience. Gloomily Beth noted that every word he spoke added significantly to the case against James Smith.

She rose reluctantly to her feet when it was time to cross-examine him. After listening to the congressman's crisp testimony, she had a horrible suspicion that cross-examination might only make his evidence sound more convincing. Nevertheless, for the sake of her client, she had an obligation to try to shake his story.

"Congressman Caine, the arresting police officer has reported that there was no sign of actual damage to your apartment door. What makes you so certain that James Smith was planning to smash your lock and burglarize your apartment?"

"He had a crowbar in his hands, which was raised above his head ready to smash down onto something. Since he was standing outside my door and the crowbar was aimed at my door handle, it seemed reasonable to assume he was planning to break into my apartment. If he hadn't been holding the crowbar over his head, he'd have been able to get to his gun more quickly and I'd never have been able to disarm him."

Several jurors were unconsciously nodding in silent approval as the congressman gave his explanation, and Beth quickly abandoned that particular line of questioning. Proving that Luke Caine was a hero would hardly advance James Smith's cause.

"Congressman, you've identified my client as the young man you saw preparing to burglarize your apartment. Interrupting an attempted robbery is a frightening experience for law-abiding citizens and it's easy to make mistakes. Why are you so positive that James Smith is the young man who threatened you last April?"

Luke Caine's voice remained solemn, but his expression was oddly sympathetic as he answered her. "James and I had plenty of time to get to know one another, Counselor. We triggered an alarm system on my front door while we were struggling for possession of the gun, so I sat on him while we waited for the police to arrive. We were eyeball to eyeball on the hall carpet for twenty minutes, and believe me, James Smith is the man who attacked me. There's no possibility of an error in my identification."

Beth hadn't expected to win the case, but Luke Caine's testimony sealed her client's fate. The jurors, like other urban dwellers, were tired of violence against law-abiding citizens and obviously thought that the congressman deserved a medal for disarming his gun-toting attacker. They reached their verdict of guilty in record time, and the judge firmly rejected her plea that James should be sent to a juvenile detention center. James was sentenced to a jail term in one of the city's overcrowded adult prisons.

"I'm sorry, James," Beth said, gathering her papers together as the police escort arrived to take him away. She had no doubt that her client was guilty, and yet she felt somehow that she had failed him—that all his life the system had been failing him. "You know my office address. Write to me if you think there's anything I can do to help."

James smiled, looked at her directly for the first time since she'd taken on the case. "Don't you trouble yourself none, lawyer lady. There's worse places than jail, and man, I done been to them all. I decided I'm gonna learn me to read while I'm away."

She touched him lightly on the arm. "You do that, please. Good luck, James."

She felt a sharp irrational jolt of pleasure when she discovered that Luke Caine was waiting for her outside the courtroom. He smiled—a heart-stopping, vote-winning, thousand-watt smile—as soon as he spotted her.

"I'm going somewhere air-conditioned to buy a long cold drink. Would you join me, Counselor?"

She hesitated, her instinctive attraction at war with her frustration over the outcome of the case. "Please come," he said. "I'd like to explain a few things about James Smith."

"All right, then. Thank you."

He took her to a bar that was blessedly cool and not very crowded at that late afternoon hour. The drinks they ordered arrived swiftly, complete with a fresh bowl of peanuts. From the deferential air of their waiter, Beth deduced that Congressman Caine was rarely kept waiting and always got peanuts with his drinks.

"Here's to you, Counselor Elizabeth Faulkner," he said, raising his glass. "And here's to ice-cold drinks and functioning air-conditioning." He leaned back in his chair, loosening his tie and unfastening the top button of his shirt. "What do your friends call you, Counselor?"

"Beth," she mumbled, burying her nose in her glass of white wine. Back in Kentucky, where she'd known everybody in her community almost from the day she was born, she'd never needed to exchange small talk, but during her years at the University of Virginia law school she'd learned to be pretty good at social chitchat. That afternoon, however, she found herself tongue-tied.

"Beth, I was watching you in court this afternoon and I know the outcome of that case upset you. I want you to understand why I pressed charges against James Smith."

She looked up, startled. "He threatened you with a gun, Mr. Caine. Isn't that reason enough? The sentence disturbed me somewhat, but I'm not such a bleeding heart that I think poverty is an automatic excuse for criminal behavior."

"My name's Luke," he said softly. "And I pressed charges against James Smith because he was higher than a kite the day he attacked me. If I hadn't immobilized him, he'd have gone somewhere else, and God knows who his next victim might have been."

"There's no need for you to explain your actions to me, Luke. I've read the police reports. I accept the fact that my client was guilty."

"Beth, how long has it been since you passed your bar exams?"

She stiffened, immediately defensive. "Several months," she said tautly, then stared down into her glass. "I know I'm still inexperienced in a courtroom. That's why I have the feeling I let James Smith down. What chance is he going to have to make something of his life now? He's seventeen years old and already society's written him off as a no-hoper."

Reaching out, Luke covered her hand in a gesture that was unexpectedly comforting. "I think James still has a chance," he said. "Maybe a better one than you think. Like you, Beth, I'm a lawyer by training, and I worked five years in the district attorney's office in Providence before I ran for political office. I'm speaking from hard-won practical experience when I tell you that our prison system isn't quite as bad as it's made out to be. Yes, our jails are overcrowded.

Yes, there's too much violence inside our jails. Yes, the inmates spend too much time staring at the walls instead of doing something constructive. But the fact is most juvenile offenders come out of jail healthier than when they went in, and close to twenty percent of them come out with more education and a higher job-skill level. James Smith was orphaned when he was five. He's been living on the street since he was twelve. He probably hasn't eaten three balanced meals a day any time in his entire life. You saw the doctor's report, so you know he has TB. He's also been pumping dope into himself so long that he's forgotten when he first got high. A prison sentence actually offers him the best chance he has to get his life together."

"If he doesn't get gang raped first," she said bitterly.

"You've seen how street kids survive," Luke replied quietly. "Do you think he'd be less likely to suffer abuse out on the street?"

She realized suddenly that Luke was right. Life in prison was always grim and occasionally violent, but it was safer than the streets. She glanced up at him, smiling slightly.

"Have you ever thought of becoming a salesman?" she asked. "I think you'd do a fabulous job of selling umbrellas and raincoats to desert sheikhs."

His gaze touched briefly on her mouth. "How about selling you on the idea of eating dinner with me?"

She had no premonition of impending disaster, only a delicious sensation of warmth uncurling smoothly in the pit of her stomach. "I'm already sold," she said breathlessly. "I'd love to have dinner with you, Luke."

They saw each other every day for the next three weeks. They dined together in some of Washington's finest restaurants, they drove into the countryside for weekend picnics, they spent Saturday afternoons touring the art galleries and museums and they spent hours exchanging intimate reminiscences about their childhoods and their years in college.

When they were apart Beth felt an unbearable ache of loneliness. When they were together she felt an odd mixture of delirious anticipation and delightful familiarity. It didn't matter if their picnic was rained out or the museum was stuffy, for when she was with Luke the whole world seemed vibrant with color and excitement. For the first time in her life, she had met somebody she wanted to confide in. She told Luke all about her family. She poured out stories about how they had been Kentucky miners for generations and how she was the first college graduate. She explained how she'd won a partial scholarship to law school and, her voice husky with affection, how her brothers and sisters-in-law had scraped together the balance of her tuition money. Wanting Luke to understand the close bonds of love among the members of her family, she chattered happily about her two teenage nephews and three young nieces, somehow convinced he would find their antics every bit as enthralling as she did.

Luke didn't talk much about his family, but he did confide some of the frustrations he had experienced working in the district attorney's office and his reasons for seeking election to the House of Representatives. His work in Providence had helped to crystallize some of his ideas about cutting crime and revitalizing inner-city neighborhoods, and he was determined to win a forum that would enable him to put his ideas into action. He made no secret of the fact that he had set his sights on a Senate seat some time in the near future. He was thirty-four, one year away from the minimum age for a senator, and Beth had little doubt that he would achieve his goal long before he was forty.

Rhode Island sent only two representatives to Congress, and Luke, starting his fourth consecutive term, was already well-known in Washington. Beth was secretly intrigued by the attention they often attracted when they were out together. It was fun going places with an almost-celebrity. On one memorable occasion, a journalist snapped their picture as they were leaving the opening of an art show, and the photo appeared the next day in the society columns of a Washington newspaper.

Congressman Luke Caine, Chairman of the House Select Committee on Organized Crime, obviously had his mind on more pleasant statistics than the latest crime figures when he escorted Elizabeth Faulkner, new recruit at the public defender's office, to the exhibition of French impressionist art at the Corcoran Gallery.

Beth read the copy beneath the photograph twice, then half-amused at her own lack of sophistication, bought three extra copies of the paper, cut out the picture with its accompanying blurb and sent it home to her family.

"We didn't hardly recognize you in them fancy clothes," Wayne wrote back. "But they sure do suit you. Mom says to tell you your hair needs cutting. Your curls were plumb over your face in that picture."

Only one part of her relationship with Luke failed to satisfy Beth. For some reason their closeness didn't extend to physical intimacy. She was too shy and too inexperienced to know how to demonstrate her willingness to make love, and Luke, far from trying to talk her into bed, rarely touched her. He kissed her good-night, of course—light, superficial kisses that left her burning with frustrated desire. Sometimes he would put his arm casually around her shoulders, and once, when they had been lying on the bank of the river after a picnic lunch, he ran his fingers through her hair then pulled her into his arms and crushed her briefly against his chest. She felt his arousal, and for a few blissful moments she thought he would kiss her properly. But in the end he rolled away and, standing up, made some excuse for them to go back to the car. Beth began seriously to consider call-

ing her former college roommate—an enterprising young
woman who had changed fiancés three times before her
twenty-first birthday—and asking for some practical advice in seduction techniques. Something about her own behavior was clearly lacking.

One Sunday, a little more than three weeks after they had
first met, Luke was unusually silent as they toured a special
exhibition at the National Portrait Gallery. The Gallery was
displaying pictures of all the women who had graced the
covers of *Time* magazine, and Beth found the photographs
fascinating.

"If you're a woman, I guess the easiest way to make the
cover of *Time* is to be born a queen or to marry a prince,"
she said as they emerged onto the steps of the Gallery.
Laughing, she added, "I think that exhibit just persuaded
me to start a new campaign for passage of the Equal Rights
Amendment. Surely by now there ought to be one or two
female power brokers in America apart from Nancy Rea-
gan! Can I interest you in my lobbying efforts, Congressman Caine?"

He didn't smile as she'd expected. He looked at her with
almost grim intensity, then raised his arm to summon a
passing cab.

"I have to go back to Rhode Island tomorrow," he announced abruptly. "In fact I should have been back there
three weeks ago."

Her heart gave a painful little lurch and she had to swal-
low hard over the lump that suddenly formed in the back of
her throat. Washington without Luke already seemed impossible to visualize.

"I'm sorry," she said, not meeting his eyes. "I'll...miss
you."

"Will you?" He paused for a minute, then said flatly,
"Come back to my apartment tonight, Beth."

She knew exactly what he was suggesting, and her throat constricted with a confused mixture of desire and panic. The cab drew up alongside the curb and he opened the door. "What address shall I give the driver?" he asked evenly.

She expelled her breath on a tight nervous sigh. "Yours."

He crooked his finger under her chin, brushing a brief hard kiss across her mouth. "Thank you," he said.

They spoke little during the drive across town, and she was shaking with nerves by the time they entered his apartment. She glanced around the room, wishing she could think of something witty to say. Unfortunately, even if she hadn't been paralyzed with fright, her knowledge of interior design was pretty much limited to Student Sordid and Sears Catalog Special, and she had no idea what style or period Luke's living room furniture belonged to. Even to her untrained eye, however, it was obviously expensive.

"It's, um, very nice," she said finally. "Your decorative scheme, I mean."

"I'm glad you approve. My mother did it for me. Would you like something to drink?"

"Some white wine if you have it."

"It's in the fridge. If you'll excuse me for a minute, I'll get it."

He left the room, and she walked nervously to one of the windows and stood there awkwardly, looking out onto a row of rooftops as she wondered what she ought to do next. Her experience in grand seduction scenes was unfortunately nil, and although her fantasy life had taken on whole new dimensions since she'd met Luke, her fantasies didn't provide much help in the present situation. It was one thing to imagine lying naked in Luke's arms as he rained kisses across her trembling body. It was altogether another matter to visualize the process by which they would progress to the bedroom. The act of getting her clothes off began to loom in her mind as the most monumental of obstacles. She was wearing control-top panty hose, she remembered suddenly. How in the world was a woman supposed to shrug sexily out of elasticized panty hose? Why in the world hadn't she worn her frilly new garter belt and a pair of stockings?

"Here's your wine."

She jumped when she heard Luke's voice. "Th-thank you." She almost grabbed it from him in her relief at having something to do with her hands. She had gulped down half the contents of the glass before he reached out and removed it from her clasp.

He put his arm around her waist and gently urged her toward the brown velvet sofa. When they were sitting down, he cupped his hands around her chin and tilted her face toward his.

For a long moment he looked at her in silence, his gray eyes dark with tenderness. "I love you, Beth," he said softly. "You're far and away the most honest and beautiful woman I've ever met."

"I love you, too," she said shyly. She was wildly, deliriously certain that the words were true, and she leaned forward to caress his cheek, not caring that her love must have been revealed in every quivering line of her body.

He captured her hand against his cheek, twisting his head to press a swift kiss into her palm, then bent to cover her mouth with his. Her heart began to thud urgently in her chest, and her body gave a little shudder of irrepressible longing as her arms crept hesitantly around his neck.

Luke gave a groan that was half sigh, half laugh as he pulled her tightly into his arms. "Oh God, Beth, I want you so much," he murmured. Suddenly his mouth was no longer soft and undemanding, but hot and urgent as he moved against hers, compelling her to part her lips and accept the fierce thrust of his tongue. Warm waves of pleasure drifted through Beth's body. She ached with a need that was almost unbearable in its intensity, and she pressed against

Luke, wanting some response from him that she was still too inexperienced to name. Instinctively she rubbed her hips against his body, desperately seeking the more intimate contact she craved.

She was startled when he pushed her away, his hands so tight on her arms that she winced. He was breathing errati-cally and his eyes were hazy with unmistakable desire. "What is it?" she asked hesitantly. "Is something wrong?"

"I don't know," he said ruefully, cradling her head against his chest. "Maybe. Beth, this is the first time you've ever made love, isn't it?"

"Yes," she whispered. "Do you...do you mind, Luke?"

"No. How can you ask such a question?" She heard the hint of rueful laughter in his voice. "The problem is that this is a first for me, too. I've never made love to a virgin." The laughter in his voice deepened. "In fact, as far as I know, I've never even spoken to a twenty-four-year-old virgin. As a species, they aren't thick on the ground in this city."

She felt her cheeks grow hot, but the tenderness in his eyes protected her from any real feeling of embarrassment. "My roommate in college always said that I could claim a record as the western world's oldest virgin, but my scholarships required a minimum B-plus average, and I was just too busy passing exams and keeping up my grades to have time to fall in love."

He traced his thumb softly over the outline of her mouth. "And you never considered the possibility of going to bed with a man you didn't love?"

"No, I guess I didn't. The town I come from is pretty conservative in its moral values, and I suppose a lot of those values brushed off on me. I wanted to be in love the first time I went to bed with someone."

His expression took on a fleeting vulnerability. "Beth, there's a definite limit to my nobility, and I've just about reached it. If you don't say no right now, I won't be able to stop what's happening between us. Are you sure you want to do this?''

"I'm sure," she said. She looked at him steadily, the beginnings of a smile curving her lips. "The truth is that I've been waiting at least two weeks for you to seduce me. I was beginning to give up hope."

"The devil you were! You might have told me! I could have saved myself forty-seven very long and very cold showers."

"Forty-seven?" she murmured teasingly.

"Uh-huh. Morning and night every day since we met. You, my sweet Beth, have a great deal to repay me for. It's a wonder I didn't develop pneumonia."

All laughter faded as he gathered her into his arms and kissed her again. His hands found the zipper of her dress and slid it slowly downward. She felt cool air strike her back as he eased her dress down to her waist. Then he cupped her breasts in his hands, and the coolness changed instantly to a burning scorching heat.

She never could remember precisely how Luke undressed her. Somehow she was standing up, and her dress was on the floor, a crumpled pool of cotton at her feet. His jacket, shirt and tie were similarly discarded. Effortlessly Luke swept her into his arms and carried her into the bedroom. He put her on the bed and, lying down beside her, held her so close that she could feel the strong beat of his heart throbbing against her breasts. As he trailed kisses all the way from her throat to her mouth, a tide of desire ripped through her, suspending thought, leaving only sensation in its wake.

She didn't notice when Luke unclipped her bra. She was only aware of the intoxicating pleasure of having her naked breasts caressed by his mouth. She didn't notice when he eased off her hose. She was only aware of the mindless, earth-shattering delight of feeling his hand slip between her thighs, teasing her to a state of ecstatic, fevered anticipation. She met his caresses with a fierce hungry abandon, winding her arms around his neck and glorying in the confident power of his lovemaking.

She had long since forgotten the fact of her virginity, a fact that seemed almost trivial in relation to the incredible sensations Luke was creating in her body. When he finally moved to possess her, she twisted away from his kiss, rigid with the shock of unexpected pain.

He buried his face in the softness of her throat, pressing tiny comforting kisses against the throbbing pulse he discovered there. A deep shudder shook his body, and then he raised his head, gently stroking her blond curls away from her sweat-dampened forehead.

"The bad part's over now," he said softly. "Are you all right, sweetheart? I tried not to hurt you."

She had already forgotten the brief moment of pain. "Kiss me again," she whispered. "And then I'll be wonderful."

"You're already wonderful." His eyes were black with desire as he arched her hips upward, molding her thighs to the hard lithe length of his body. He claimed her mouth again, murmuring provocative enticing words of love as he caressed her. Gradually, tenderly, he brought her again to the white-hot readiness she had known before and the tempo of his movements became more urgent until, with one final kiss, he swept her away to ecstasy.

Afterward she shifted languidly on the bed, still drowsy with contentment. Her body felt light and yet fulfilled in a way it never had before. Luke's hand trailed lightly across her stomach, evoking a delightful lazy sort of pleasure. She smiled up at him, already half-asleep.

"Marry me, Beth," he said quietly.

Later, after they were married and she was about a thousand times more sophisticated, she often wondered precisely what combination of quixotic honor and sexual attraction prompted his proposal. At that moment, however, safe in the haven of his arms, she was conscious of nothing save a soaring breathtaking happiness. She loved Luke and he loved her. They had just made glorious love. It seemed only right to her that he would want to get married.

Her smile deepened and she snuggled blissfully against him. "Yes," she said, not bothering to pretend even a smidgeon of doubt or reluctance. "Let's get married soon."

His arms tightened lovingly around her, but his laughter held more than a hint of wryness. "The sex was that good, huh?"

"It was better than good."

"Mmm, well how would you feel if I demonstrated a few of my more interesting variations?" He lifted her up so that she straddled his body, the tips of her breasts just brushing his skin. "There was the one I discovered a couple of years ago, that goes something like this...."

CHAPTER FIVE

THEY WERE MARRIED six weeks later in her hometown of Mayville, Kentucky. Her father rented a navy blue suit for the occasion, having refused categorically to get himself stuffed—his words—into a tuxedo. Her mother, bursting with pride at her daughter's handsome fiancé, bought the most expensive dress in the J.C. Penney catalog and a new pair of patent leather shoes to go with it. Beth's three nieces were flower girls, her two nephews were ushers, and three hundred people—more than half the town's population—crowded into the local church to see the wedding.

Luke's mother, Ruth Caine, flew into Kentucky from Europe the day before the ceremony. She said very little and what she did say was not complimentary, but Beth, surrounded by the overflowing love of her family and friends, hardly even noticed her future mother-in-law's snobbish disapproval.

The first crack in her happiness came when she and Luke returned from their idyllic two-week honeymoon in the Bahamas. They flew into Boston's Logan Airport and were met by a chauffeur-driven car for the journey to Luke's home in Newport. Bill Decker, Luke's senior political aide and personal assistant, arrived with the chauffeur.

"Good afternoon, Mrs. Caine, how are you?" Bill didn't wait for Beth to reply before handing Luke a thick briefcase. "This is just the most important stuff, Luke. With Congress about to reconvene, you can hardly get inside your office door for the stacks of mail."

Luke opened the briefcase immediately, then turned to look at Beth. "You don't mind, darling, if I catch up on some paperwork? What with one thing and another, these past two weeks I've got pretty behind in my work." The smile in his eyes invited her to remember just what they had been doing while the urgent memorandums were piling up at his office.

"Of course it's all right." Beth smiled back. She was a career woman herself, for heaven's sake, and she understood the demands Luke's work would inevitably make upon him. She certainly had no intention whatever of becoming a nagging wife. She squeezed his hand. "You go ahead and work. I'll lean back and admire the scenery." Mischief danced in her eyes as she thought of how they had spent the previous night. "I'm a little tired anyway. I could use a quick nap."

Her mood became a little less sympathetic when they arrived at Luke's ocean-front home—euphemistically named Cobden Farm—and he still ignored her. Looking wryly at the sweeping lawns, the ornamental pond, the iron-balustraded patios and the direct access to the private beach, Beth thought that she had rarely seen anything less farmlike than this. She estimated that Mayville's entire Main Street would fit quite comfortably into one of the property's side lawns. For the first time it occurred to her that Luke had been extremely reticent about discussing his family and his family connections. She was so used to living on minuscule amounts of money that she had never really stopped to consider how wealthy Luke might actually be. From her humble perspective, a congressman's salary and allowances seemed huge, and she had never thought to question whether Luke actually lived on his government salary. As she looked at the mellow brick facade of Cobden Farm and saw afternoon sun reflected off dozens of shining lead-glass windows, it dawned on Beth that she had been incredibly naive. Her husband was not only a hardworking member of the House of Representatives, but was also an extremely rich man.

Luke obviously saw no reason to comment on the size or the splendor of his home, and with Bill Decker glued to his side, Beth felt this wasn't an appropriate moment to point out that she had never before in her life entered a private house that possessed more than two bathrooms. She trotted along beside Luke as, still preoccupied with Bill's discussion of some technical point of legislation, he swept into the hallway. She gritted her teeth and willed herself not to feel small and insignificant as she surveyed the hallway, which she estimated grimly was approximately two and a half times as large as her parents' entire house.

Ruth Caine was waiting at the foot of a huge oaken staircase, her beringed fingers resting elegantly on the carved post. She looked, Beth ruefully decided, alarmingly like one of the less friendly characters from a nineteenth-century Gothic novel.

"Luke dearest!" His mother's penetrating aristocratic tones pierced the gloom of the dark-paneled hallway. She strode across the gleaming parquet floor, the soft drift of her silk dress subtly at odds with the steely determination of her manner.

Luke broke off his conversation with Bill Decker at last. "Hello, Mother," he said, kissing her briefly. "You're looking well."

"And so are you, dear." Ruth Caine patted her immaculate much-sprayed hairdo and looked pointedly at Beth. "But you look a little frazzled, my dear. The Caribbean sun always has such an unfortunate effect on pale complexions."

Beth was immediately conscious of her sun-flushed cheeks and peeling nose. She had fallen asleep on the balcony of their room after making love with Luke, and the sun had wreaked havoc with her fair skin.

"I think Beth looks even more beautiful than usual," Luke said, putting his arm around her shoulders and hugging her to his side. "Her hair is like a cloud of golden sunshine and her cheeks are like roses. As for her nose..." He paused, then grinned and dropped a kiss on the bright red peeling skin. "Well, I guess makeup can cover a multitude of sins."

Bill Decker coughed and Ruth Caine's smile froze around the edges. "Whatever you say, Luke. Fortunately there's time for her to take a shower and change before our dinner guests arrive."

Startled, Beth glanced up at Luke. "Are we having guests for dinner tonight? But how can we? I mean, we haven't organized anything—"

"Naturally the housekeeper and I have made all the necessary arrangements," the older woman said repressively. "It's only a dozen or so guests, nothing at all to get worked up about. Please follow me, Beth. Luke has a great deal to do, and we ladies must leave the menfolk to their work. I'll show you to your room."

Luke gave her another hug. "Go with Mother, honey. She'll enjoy showing you around the house, and if you're tired, you can lie down for half an hour or so. Our guests won't be arriving much before eight. I'll meet you upstairs as soon as I'm through with Bill."

Beth was sitting on the edge of their king-size bed, wrapped in a towel and feeling thoroughly miserable when Luke came upstairs a couple of hours later. He slung his jacket and tie onto a chair—probably a priceless Louis XV antique, Beth thought gloomily, hating its spindly gilt legs and stiff satin upholstery—and came quickly across the enormous room to the bed.

"Now that was first-class planning, Mrs. Caine," he murmured huskily, one hand going to his belt buckle as the other hand pushed the fluffy monogrammed towel away from her shoulders. "What a waste of time it would have been if you'd put your clothes on!"

She caught his hand just before it claimed possession of her breast. "Luke, why didn't you tell me about this house and the servants and the dinner party and everything?"

"What do you mean, honey? I told you that I lived right on the ocean in a house that has belonged to my family for nearly a hundred years."

"But somehow you forgot to tell me that it was only slightly smaller than the White House, with a servant lurking in every second corner!"

He shrugged, looking faintly embarrassed. "Hell, Beth, it's just a house. I've lived in it all my life and I guess I don't think about how big it is."

"And what about the dinner party? Luke, I'm not used to entertaining a dozen guests at the drop of a hat. I'm afraid I'm not going to be much help as a political hostess, at least not until I get more accustomed to your kind of lifestyle."

"Sweetheart, the dinner party was as much a surprise to me as it was to you. I wish my mother had left us alone just for tonight, but she likes to entertain and we probably have guests five nights a week. But it's no big deal. Believe me, I didn't marry you simply to get myself a hostess. That was the last thing I needed. My mother's been taking care of my political entertaining for years."

Beth found Luke's explanation less than reassuring. The prospect of formal dinner parties five nights out of seven, with her mother-in-law presiding at the head of the table, was not very appealing. Her doubts must have shown, for Luke caught her face between his hands and looked at her searchingly.

"Beth, the important thing for you to remember is that Cobden Farm is your home now. You can do whatever you want to do here, be whatever you want to be. If you feel like throwing out the furniture in our bedroom and redecorating, then go ahead and do that. If you want to make changes downstairs—well, as a courtesy to my mother I'd appreciate it if you'd check with her first—but you're the mistress of this house now, Beth, and you must do whatever you need to do to feel comfortable here."

She traced the pattern on one of the exquisite lace panels set into the bedspread. "Does, um, does your mother always live in this house, Luke?"

"No, of course not. I told you before we were married that my mother would be spending part of every year with us, but she has her own apartment in Paris and a house in northern Florida where she spends most of the winter." He kissed her lingeringly, pulling open the towel and clasping her hard against his chest. "Don't worry, Beth," he said hoarsely. "We'll have lots of time to be alone together."

Later, she was to realize that their entire married life would follow the pattern established on that very first day, but in the delirious happiness of her relationship with Luke, it was several months before she admitted to herself that, though their rapport in the bedroom was transcendental, the rest of their lives followed virtually separate paths.

Whatever Ruth Caine's normal routine might have been, during the first winter of her son's marriage, she showed no signs of planning to depart for Florida. On the contrary, she invited her sister, Mary, for an extended vacation, and Beth found herself more than ever an outsider.

Mary was married to Giuseppe Bellini, a prosperous lawyer with offices throughout the neighboring states, as well as Rhode Island. He came for dinner one Sunday, and Beth found him a pleasant guest—plump, cheerful and disarmingly anxious to include her in the conversation.

"Call me Uncle Peppe," he said expansively as soon as they were introduced. He held Beth's hand much too long and kissed her on the cheek enthusiastically. "And you must call my wife Aunt Maria. What is all this nonsense of Mrs. Bellini? You are part of the family now, and that means we care for each other, no?"

Beth could hardly say that this was the first time she'd ever been asked to call anyone in Luke's family, other than Luke, by their first name, so she smiled politely. "Aunt Maria?" she questioned. "I thought your wife's name was Mary, Uncle Peppe."

"It is," Ruth Caine interjected coldly. "And Mary is a good solid Anglo-Saxon name, not like Maria."

Uncle Peppe's eyes twinkled and he slipped Beth a surreptitious wink before turning an expression of bland innocence on Ruth. "Ah, but your sister likes me to call her Maria, isn't that so, my pet?"

"Yes, yes, of course." Aunt Maria was a fluttery nervous woman who seemed perpetually anxious to please everybody. "But it's quite all right if my sister calls me Mary."

When Ruth announced that dinner was ready, Uncle Peppe immediately jumped to his feet and offered his arm to Beth. "I am the oldest man here," he said. "So it's my privilege to escort the prettiest woman. Go away, Luke, and find somebody else to entertain you. For this evening, Beth is all mine."

After such outrageous flattery it wasn't difficult for Beth to decide that Uncle Peppe was her favorite new relative. The fact that her mother-in-law so obviously disapproved of him merely added to her feelings. Uncle Peppe had the same sort of warmth and openheartedness she was used to in her own family, and it was a tremendous relief to be with somebody so uncomplicated after enduring weeks of Ruth Caine's rigid formality.

She passed her opinion on to Luke when they were in bed that night. "I enjoyed meeting Uncle Peppe," she said. "Why doesn't he come to visit more often?"

If she had been paying more attention she would have sensed the odd hesitation before he replied. "Uncle Peppe travels a lot, and my mother doesn't encourage his visits."

"No, I'm sure she doesn't. First generation Italian immigrants are hardly her style."

"My mother has a lot of outdated prejudices," Luke said quietly. "But that isn't why she objects to Uncle Peppe."

Beth yawned. She had drunk three glasses of wine at dinner, one more than her usual limit, and she was deliciously sleepy. She snuggled closer to Luke's body and trailed her hand suggestively down the flat plane of his stomach.

There was no more discussion of Uncle Peppe that night.

Beth quickly relinquished her few tentative efforts to take control of the Cobden Farm household. She had no desire to engage in a pitched battle with her mother-in-law and, in truth, was somewhat relieved to be free of the obligation to supervise a domestic staff of three full-time workers and numerous part-time ones. Her skills definitely lay in other directions.

The household routine, she soon discovered, was designed to maximize Luke's efficiency. He was chairman of the family's machine manufacturing company, as well as the best known politician in the state, and his schedule was almost frightening in the demands it placed upon him. He was often in Washington, of course, and when he was home it seemed to Beth that Cobden Farm was literally beseiged by aides, employees, constituents and party officials, all anxious to add to his workload. She learned to hate the sight of Bill Decker and his overflowing briefcase.

She had always intended to return to work as soon as she could find a suitable job, and Luke's hectic schedule merely confirmed her decision. He was entirely supportive when she told him that she had applied for a vacant spot in the local district attorney's office.

"That's great, Beth," he said. "You're a gifted conscientious lawyer and you should put your training and your talents to work."

Later, when she told him she'd been awarded the job, they went out for a private celebratory dinner, then came home and spent the rest of the night making wild delirious love.

Beth had always been sure Kristin was conceived that night. Even now, when she knew that her feelings for Luke had been based on nothing but falsehoods, she was always secretly glad that her child had been conceived at least with the illusion of love.

She waited until a doctor confirmed she was pregnant before she told Luke the news. He had just come out of the shower and was crossing to his dressing room, ready to outfit himself for one of the endless formal dinners that always seemed to be taking place at Cobden Farm. His wet hair gleamed in the lamplight and droplets of water glistened on his tanned muscular shoulders. A sudden weakness seized Beth's knees at the sight of him.

"I'm going to have a baby." She blurted out the words, unable to keep them secret for another second. She had meant to whisper them provocatively over champagne, but suddenly she felt so full of love that the news could no longer be contained inside her.

He froze in the middle of a step, then turned and swept her into his arms. "Darling, Beth! A baby! It's what I've wanted for us more than anything else in the world." He stroked his hand wonderingly over her stomach. "My child growing inside you. Are you pleased, Beth? You don't wish we'd waited a bit longer?"

"Of course not," she said softly. "I'm thrilled."

"Do you feel all right?" His voice became husky with anxiety. "You've been working so hard these past few weeks. You haven't been overdoing it, have you? Aren't you supposed to feel sick or something?''

She laughed. ''I feel fine, just a little sleepy in the evenings, that's all. The doctor says I'm strong as a horse and there's no reason I shouldn't continue working at the D.A.'s office for another six months at least.''

He continued to stroke his hand gently over her abdomen. ''When is the baby due?''

''September.''

''Just in time for our first wedding anniversary. Oh Beth, I'm so happy! You can't imagine how much I've wanted you to have my child.'' He kissed her gently on the forehead. ''We have a lot of planning to do, I guess. Have you thought about what you'll do when the baby's born?''

''Not really. There hasn't been much time for planning. From the articles I've read, I think it would probably be better if I stayed home for the first year after the baby's born, but I expect I'll go back to work eventually. After all there's plenty of domestic help here and we could hire a really good nanny. Would you mind?''

''No, of course I wouldn't mind. Besides, that's more your decision than mine.'' His voice thickened with emotion as he lightly skimmed her hair with shaking fingers. ''To hell with the dinner guests. Tonight we're going somewhere quiet and intimate, just the two of us.''

''Two and a quarter of us,'' she whispered, smiling at him, though her eyes were misty with tears.

LOOKING BACK, Beth sometimes thought that was the last really meaningful conversation she ever had with Luke. It was on the very next day, while she was at work, that she first discovered the truth about charming, good-natured Uncle Peppe. Joe Castle, a notorious loan shark, was being indicted for murder and Giuseppe Bellini was listed as his defense attorney.

Her colleague who was prosecuting the case grunted as he saw the listing. "Bellini, of course. Crooked bastard. Who the hell else would a piece of slime like Castle choose to defend him?"

His question was rhetorical, but Beth couldn't help responding. "What's wrong with Giuseppe Bellini?"

Her colleague smiled angrily. "Nothing, I guess, if you like crooked lawyers who are working for every organized criminal on the eastern seaboard."

"Even organized criminals are entitled to a good defense lawyer."

"Yeah, but Bellini doesn't just front for them in court. He's in on all the backstairs deals as well. He has an ocean-going yacht and a private jet that he sure as hell didn't pay for out of legitimate after-tax earnings. I tried to get the evidence to indict him once, but he'd covered his tracks too well, and the D.A. decided we didn't have a case that would stand up in court."

Uncle Peppe was the only person who had made any attempt to make Beth feel welcome in her new home and was the only relative of Luke's she really liked. Now it seemed that even he was not the warm, genuinely kind person he appeared on the surface. Beth felt truly disheartened.

She confronted Luke with her information as soon as she got home that night. For once, Bill Decker's pleas that Luke was too busy to be disturbed had no effect on her determination.

He didn't deny the truth of what she had heard, but he told her point blank that she was being foolish if she seriously thought she could prosecute Uncle Peppe for corruption. "You're being naive, Beth," he said tersely. "The D.A.'s office has investigated him before and come up empty. If you visualize yourself as a white knight, forget it. If you think you're going to ride into his office on your noble charger and emerge with the evidence to convict him, you're seriously underestimating the difficulties."

"Maybe, but at least I could give it a try instead of tacitly condoning his criminal behavior."

Luke stood up, tension etching hard lines between his nose and his mouth. "I don't condone Peppe's past behavior, either, if that's what you're suggesting."

"You invited him to dinner last month, and he's coming to another party next weekend."

"Peppe is married to my aunt," Luke said quietly. "To my mother's only sister. The invitations are for their sake, not because I'm particularly seeking Peppe's company."

"But how can you even speak to him so politely, knowing that he's made his money by betraying the ethics of his profession?"

"For a lawyer, you sling accusations around pretty indiscriminately, Beth. Peppe has never been convicted of corruption. In fact, he's never been convicted of any crime whatsoever."

"Well, maybe it's time somebody worked on getting the evidence to convict him! Lawyers are supposed to uphold the law, not find clever ways to work around it!" She slammed out of his office before he had a chance to reply.

She pursued her investigation vigorously, working with some local law-enforcement officers who were as anxious as she was to clamp down on organized crime. They built their case slowly, without any dramatic breakthroughs, but by the end of April she felt she definitely had something—not enough to ask the D.A. for an indictment, but certainly enough to go to him and ask for a full-scale, no-holds-barred investigation.

She hadn't discussed her plans with Luke. For one thing, he was spending so much time in Washington that they rarely met except late at night in the darkness of the bedroom. But one Saturday night they skipped dinner and went to bed early. They lay comfortably twined in each other's arms, catching up on each other's activities. Hesitantly, worrying about how the news would affect Aunt Maria and the rest of the family, Beth confided that she was almost ready to present a case against Uncle Peppe to the district attorney.

She felt Luke's body stiffen before he rolled away from her. "Beth, would you please accept my word that this isn't a good time to prosecute the case against Uncle Peppe?"

"I can't do that," she said, her throat aching with suppressed tension. "I understand how you must feel about Aunt Maria. I even understand why you're worried about your political career. But Luke, can't you please try to see things from my point of view? How can I prosecute other criminals convincingly when my own uncle by marriage is allowed to get away with twisting the law to suit his own corrupt purposes?"

"Beth, if you've ever trusted me in anything, trust me that it would be better for everybody if you dropped this investigation."

She got up and pulled on her dressing gown with shaking fingers. "Personal trust has nothing to do with this, Luke. It's a matter of professional integrity. I'm a lawyer working in the district attorney's office, and Peppe is a suspected criminal. I'm going downstairs to the library to find something to read. Don't wait up for me."

Less than a week later the D.A. called her into his office.

"You're looking blooming," he said, smiling as he nodded at the bulge beginning to appear under her loose blouse. "How is the Dekatur case going?"

She filled him in on the details and was pleased when he complimented her on her careful work. "By the way," he said as they walked toward his office door. "I hear that you've been putting in some overtime, working up a case against Giuseppe Bellini."

She tensed. "Yes, I have. But I've kept up with all the cases officially assigned to me."

He patted her kindly on the shoulder. "Beth, nobody's questioning your hard work, just your judgment. It's my responsibility to decide what prosecutions we go after. Drop the investigation on Bellini, will you?"

"I can't do that," she said. "I think we could easily work up an indictment. Another few weeks and I'll have information—"

"Beth, this is a direct order. Drop the investigation on Giuseppe Bellini or you're out of a job."

Beth wasn't sure what would have happened if she'd gone home and found Luke waiting for her that night. Fortunately he was in Washington, and she retreated to the lonely sanctuary of their bedroom and paced the floor, trying to decide what she ought to do next. She wished there was somebody she could ask for advice. For the first time she realized that, though the house was filled with people, there wasn't a single person she could call a friend. Mrs. Caine actively disliked her, the servants ignored her, and Luke's aides viewed her simply as an inconvenient rival for their employer's attention. She had met dozens of new people since her marriage, but she considered them all Luke's friends and acquaintances. She had never attempted to turn any of them into her friends. Now, when it was already too late, she wished she had made more of an effort to establish some local contacts. She realized belatedly that she had been far too willing to lose herself in the seductive enchantment of her husband's lovemaking.

Luke arrived home at lunchtime on Saturday. "How are you, sweetheart? How was the doctor's visit?"

"Fine, except that I gained five pounds last week. The doctor made me swear off desserts until September. When the baby's born and you visit me in the hospital, don't bring flowers, bring chocolate fudge ripple ice cream. I'm already suffering all the symptoms of acute withdrawal."

He laughed, brushing a kiss across her cheek. "It's a deal." He walked into the closet. "How are things at the office?" he called out.

His question sounded casual, but some new awareness, some previously untested sixth sense, alerted Beth to the fact that it was nowhere near as casual as it seemed. *Why would it be?* she thought bitterly. *He's undoubtedly checking up to see if the D.A.'s done what he was told to do.*

"Fine," she said. "Everything's going very smoothly. The D.A. complimented me on the way I'm handling the Dekatur case." Luke emerged from the closet, pulling a sweater over his head. She turned away and stared determinedly out of the window. "The sea looks quite blue today, doesn't it? How long do you think it will be before we can go swimming?"

"By the end of the month if you don't mind freezing your butt off. Mid-July if you want to be comfortably warm."

She forced a smile. "I guess I'll wait for mid-July." She patted her stomach. "Junior here tells me he doesn't like cold water."

He came up behind her and clasped his hands around her expanding waistline. "Since when did he become a he?"

"The obstetrician says the fetal heartbeat is very slow and that a slow fetal heartbeat usually means a boy."

He grinned. "Sounds like an old wives' tale to me. Let's go and get lunch, shall we? I'll eat cottage cheese and carrot sticks and refuse dessert just to prove what a sympathetic husband I am."

Beth followed the D.A.'s orders and on Monday telephoned Lieutenant Landers, the detective who had been working with her on the Bellini investigation. Crisply, without revealing any hint of her inner feelings, she told him that staffing pressures within the D.A.'s office meant that they could no longer support a probe of an individual not directly accused of any specific crime.

She learned later that her refusal to cooperate did not, in fact, dissuade the local police from continuing their own investigation. Early in June, Lieutenant Landers brought her conclusive documentary evidence showing that the Timberline Construction Corporation had bilked the state of close to a million dollars on substandard highway and bridge construction. Timberline was a local company that employed Giuseppe Bellini as its senior legal counsel. Glancing over the corporate documents, Beth saw that Luke Cobden Caine had recently been appointed as one of its senior directors. Torn by conflicting loyalties, she agonized over what she should do. After days of soul-searching and nights of insomnia, she agreed with Lieutenant Landers that she should renew her investigation. Within weeks, she and the lieutenant had uncovered sufficient evidence to indict several local government officials on charges of corruption.

The police investigation had also uncovered evidence that Timberline Corporation was working in close cooperation with some powerful personage in Washington D.C. According to the police, an unnamed Washington contact was paying off federal highway inspectors, arranging the shipment of substandard building materials and generally greasing the wheels of corruption to insure smooth passage for the local operators. Only the name of the Washington contact remained unknown.

Finally, on July 15, a detective who had infiltrated Peppe's law office informed Beth that Peppe and a local building inspector, already identified as being on the take, were scheduled to meet the Washington contact at the Greenhouse Restaurant, off Highway 195 over the state border in Massachusetts.

"Look, let me take care of covering the meeting," Beth said. "There's no reason for you to blow your cover, and if Peppe spots you at the restaurant, there's a good chance he'll cancel the meeting before the Washington contact ever shows."

Detective Pirelli protested, but eventually she won her point. She called Cobden Farm to let the housekeeper know she wouldn't be home for dinner, thinking even as she placed the call that Peppe's corruption was rubbing off on her. She knew very well why she had insisted on covering the assignment alone, and it had nothing to do with blowing the detective's cover.

She arrived at the restaurant shortly after seven, nearly thirty minutes before the rendezvous was scheduled to take place. She had taken the precaution of wearing a dark wig and glasses, but there was nothing she could do to conceal her pregnancy. Still, she didn't think there was much chance she would be recognized, even if Peppe happened to see her standing. The conspirators had chosen their meeting place well, she reflected. The restaurant was quite small, but the lighting was dim and the seating cunningly arranged so that almost everybody was either enclosed in a booth or screened by some sort of potted plant. She selected a seat that was close to the door and waited patiently for Uncle Peppe to show up.

At seven-twenty-five a small stir at the entrance marked the arrival of a new group of diners. Her heart pounding, her mouth dry and her palms sweating with nerves, Beth recognized one of the local building inspectors Lieutenant Landers had identified as seriously corrupt. The baby gave a sudden sharp kick when Beth saw Uncle Peppe and two men she didn't recognize follow the building inspector to a table only a few feet away from her booth. Uncle Peppe glanced up, and for a split second she thought he must have recognized her, but his glance veered immediately away, and she slunk deeper into the shadows of her booth as he looked down at his watch. He murmured something inaudible to his companions, but it was clear that they were waiting for a further arrival—obviously the infamous Washington contact.

The waitress, a perky young thing with a sweet smile, came up and asked Beth if she would like dessert. Terrified of drawing attention to herself, Beth jerked out a whispered request for coffee.

At seven-thirty-five the door swung open again, and this time two men stood silhouetted in the fluorescent lighting of the entryway. Uncle Peppe jumped up, his face a mass of cheerful smiles as he welcomed the new arrivals. One of the men was Bill Decker. The other was Luke Caine. Beth closed her eyes, feeling cold sweat break out on her forehead as she struggled with a sudden violent urge to be sick.

"Luke, I'm delighted you managed to make it. My associates have everything in order for you."

Uncle Peppe really should learn to keep his voice down, Beth thought coldly. Did they feel so safe in their sordid conspiracies that they saw no reason to whisper?

"That's good news," Luke said. Unlike Peppe he wasn't speaking loudly, but his wonderful mellow voice always carried across any room. Beth had frequently thought it was one of his greater assets as a politician.

She heard the rustling of clothing and the squish of leather as everybody sat down, then Luke's voice came again. "Bill has been very successful with his efforts in Washington this week. I think you'll all be delighted with the results of his endeavors. In fact any time you want to expand your operations, I think I could get very favorable terms for you in Pennsylvania."

Beth couldn't hear the question Luke was asked, and she had no way of guessing who was speaking, but she heard his answer with sickening painful clarity. "Oh no, Sammy, my friend! A hundred thousand buys you clearance in Rhode Island, not in Pennsylvania. Pennsylvania is a hell of a lot bigger than Rhode Island and it's going to cost you a lot more. Bill and I thought a quarter of a million would be a reasonable sum. Paid straight into that wonderful nontaxable account of mine in Switzerland.''

"Would you care for some more coffee, miss?"

Beth blinked, trying hard to make sense of the waitress's question. "I'm sorry," she said hoarsely. "What did you say?"

"Would you like some more coffee? Excuse me, miss, but are you feeling all right?"

"Yes, yes, thank you. I'm fine."

Except that I've just heard irrefutable evidence that my husband's a crook.

She pasted a smile on her shaking lips and forced herself to speak. "Could I have the check, please?"

She didn't wait for the waitress to return. She saw another party of diners preparing to leave the restaurant, and pulling a twenty-dollar bill out of her purse, she tossed it blindly onto the table. When the group passed between her and Luke, she stood up and walked out with them.

She had no conscious memory of driving back from the restaurant to Cobden Farm. When she regained full possession of her faculties, she was already back in her bedroom, throwing clothes into a suitcase.

She paused in the act of thrusting a cotton maternity dress into her case. Detective Pirelli was going to expect to hear from her, and the case would blow wide open if she disappeared without leaving him any message.

She sat down on the bed and calmly dialed his home number.

"Jason? This is Elizabeth Caine," she said as soon as the detective came on the line. "I have bad news, I'm afraid. The Washington contact didn't show tonight."

"Hell and damnation!" Detective Pirelli muttered several other choice expletives beneath his breath. "I was so sure my information was correct."

"Maybe it was. Giuseppe Bellini was there with a couple of his usual cronies and he obviously expected somebody to show. Maybe the Washington contact got delayed."

Detective Pirelli laughed bitterly. "Yeah, he probably got called to a committee meeting. How much do you bet he's the head of some Washington think tank preparing a report on organized crime?"

"Sounds quite likely to me," she said, wondering how in God's name she was managing to sound so calm. She was sweating so much that the phone kept slipping in her hands. "Justin, I should have told you before, but I'm going to take a couple of weeks off from work. This pregnancy business is more exhausting than I thought it would be."

"I've heard that one before from my wife!" This time, Detective Pirelli's laughter was entirely sympathetic. "Are you staying home if I need to contact you urgently?"

"No, I'm going to my family in Kentucky, so you should channel all your reports through the police chief. Please don't go to the D.A. until you have the evidence down cold. You know he told me that we didn't have the resources to pursue this investigation, and he wouldn't be too thrilled if he knew I'd been working on it with you."

"Don't worry. I know all about office politics. We'll keep everything under wraps."

"Thanks. And Justin...take care."

"Yeah, you too. Believe me, I'm being careful. I want to nail these bastards, but I've no intention of ending my days floating face down in the river."

It was after midnight by the time she finished her packing and crept down the back stairs to one of the little-used rear exits. She was walking through the darkened kitchen when she realized that, unless she left Luke some sort of message, the FBI might end up searching for her as a kidnap victim. She sat down at the kitchen table, suddenly overwhelmed by the urge to put her head down and weep. She didn't want to plan efficiently for her disappearance. She wanted to lie in the big bed upstairs and wait for Luke to come home. She wanted him to tell her that she hadn't really seen him bargaining with criminals in the Greenhouse Restaurant for the sake of a quarter-million-dollar payment into his Swiss bank account.

She got up, dry-eyed, and looked around for something to write on. Next to the telephone was a memo pad of pink paper, shaped and scented like a huge strawberry. She picked up a pen and wrote quickly before she had time to change her mind.

"Luke, I'm sorry, I can't live with you anymore. Beth."

She read the message through twice. As far as she could see, it said pretty much everything there was to say.

She stuck the pink paper on the fridge with a magnet and walked out of the house.

CHAPTER SIX

KRISTIN CLUNG TO BETH'S HAND as they followed Luke and Bill Decker through the airport terminal toward the baggage pickup area. Their flight had been late in arriving at Boston's Logan Airport, and it was more than seven hours since they had left the apartment in Denver. Kristin was hugging her tattered pink security blanket and sucking the ear of her teddy bear, a sure sign she was feeling nervous. Beth reflected wryly that if she had a security blanket, she'd be hugging it, too. As it was, she concentrated on trying to look a great deal calmer than she felt.

"Take care, honey," she said when Kristin stumbled getting onto the moving walkway. "Here, maybe I'd better carry you."

Luke had given the impression of being lost in conversation with Bill Decker, but he turned around immediately at the sound of Beth's voice and swung his daughter up into his arms.

Kristin wriggled in his grasp. "Me get down," she said. "Teddy wants Mama, not Man."

Luke tightened his hold on his squirming daughter, then solemnly examined the wet-eared bear. "Mmm, what do you know? You're quite right. Teddy looks sad, so of course we must give him to your mommy." He politely extracted the stuffed animal from Kristin's arms, pretending not to see her sudden frown.

"Here, Beth," he said with a bland smile. "Teddy would like you to hold him."

Kristin's blue eyes opened very wide as she watched her mother take the bear. She remained silent, not quite sure what had happened, but aware that she had been subtly outsmarted by her father. *Join the club, honey,* Beth thought ruefully.

Outside the terminal building they were met by the same chauffeur who had welcomed Beth and Luke home from their honeymoon. He seemed no happier to greet Beth on this occasion than he had been three years earlier. He nodded toward her in a minimum gesture of formal politeness, but his face broke into a smile as soon as he saw Kristin.

"She looks just like you, Mr. Caine," he said, totally ignoring the fact that Kristin's soft brown coloring was not a bit like Luke's. "She sure is the spitting image of her daddy." He produced a giant red lollipop from his pocket and held it out to Kristin with a flourish. "Welcome home, young lady. We're all delighted to have you back where you belong."

Kristin, who was almost never allowed to eat candy, accepted the lollipop with a beaming smile. She was smart enough not even to glance toward her mother. She held out the candy to Luke, and he obligingly tore off the cellophane wrapping.

"Fank you," she said, giving him one of her most dazzling and flirtatious smiles. She sucked blissfully, still avoiding her mother's eyes.

The men all laughed indulgently, while Beth gripped her hands together and resisted the urge to snatch the obnoxious red candy out of her daughter's hands. They hadn't even left the airport, she thought with a flare of resentment, and already everyone was acting as if she were irrelevant to the supervision of her own daughter. As far as Luke's household was concerned, she had always been a nonperson, and it seemed as though nothing had changed.

A porter finished stowing their luggage in the trunk of the car, and the chauffeur held open the door of the limousine. "I hope you don't mind my offering Kristin candy at this hour of the day, Mr. Caine, but it's a long ride for a little girl, and I thought a lollipop might keep her occupied."

"It was a fine idea," Luke said easily. "She has plenty of time to settle into a healthy routine tomorrow. One day of spoiling won't hurt."

Beth smiled through clenched teeth. "Especially if it's your suit Kristin throws up over," she said sweetly.

Luke grinned and carefully unwound one of his daughter's fine brown curls from the sticky candy. "She looks as if she has a pretty hardy constitution," he said, his voice low and tolerant. "And my family never has suffered from travel sickness."

Beth had often wondered how people gnashed their teeth. Now she knew. She started to point out that members of *her* family were notoriously bad travelers, but the chauffeur chose this moment to set the car in motion, and her words were lost in the sputter of the engine. Bill Decker immediately drew Luke's attention to a message that had been received direct from the White House only that morning. Luke listened attentively, although he made no attempt to relinquish his hold on his daughter.

Kristin, who knew when she was onto a good thing, continued to avoid her mother's gaze. She relaxed in Luke's arms, alternately sucking her candy and cuddling her security blanket. Every so often she would poke surreptitiously at her father's chest, as if curious about the difference between his taut muscles and her mother's soft yielding warmth. Luke must have been aware of what she was doing, but he made no comment and didn't even glance down to see what her sticky fingers were doing to his five-hundred dollar suit.

Beth sat stiffly in a corner of the limo, the teddy bear propped up on her lap, listening to the murmur of Luke's voice and willing herself not to feel jealous of Kristin's interest in her father. She forced her head to turn in the direction of the smoked-glass window, watching the familiar scenery flash by. She was surprised that so much remained unchanged.

It had been about this time of year when she and Luke returned from their honeymoon in the Bahamas. The trees lining the highway were once again austere, leafless skeletons, silhouetted against a gray, overcast sky. She swallowed hard over the sudden constriction in her throat. The scenery might be the same as it had been three years ago, but she was an entirely different woman. Dear heaven, she had been so happy the last time they had taken this drive, so naively certain she had found the love that would last her a lifetime.

Beth pulled her mouth into a hard uncompromising line. It was dangerous to think of the word *love* in connection with Luke. She must remember that the man she had fallen in love with never existed outside the realm of her imagination. She must remember that the real Luke Caine was a crook who had sold out his constituents and conspired with one of the state's most corrupt lawyers. Most of all, she must remember that she owed it to herself and Kristin to escape from him again as soon as she could. Her daughter deserved more from life than to be brought up in the corrupt, power-obsessed atmosphere of Cobden Farm.

Luke divided his attention between Kristin and his assistant, never once addressing a remark to Beth. She didn't mind her isolation, however, because it gave her a chance to put her defenses into better order. It had been difficult enough to forget how attractive Luke was when they had been a thousand miles apart. At such close quarters it was almost impossible to ignore the dynamic sensual appeal of his masculinity.

Luke didn't speak to her directly until the limo was drawing to a halt outside the main entrance to Cobden Farm. "Aunt Maria has been taking care of the house for the past couple of years," he said, turning abruptly to face Beth. "She's looking forward to seeing you again and to meeting Kristin."

Beth's face mirrored her astonishment. "But where's your mother? Why isn't she in charge of the house? I can't imagine her handing over the reins to Aunt Maria!"

"My mother's in Europe. As a matter of fact, she hasn't stayed with me for some time. Not since a couple of weeks after you left." Luke held Beth's gaze steadily, and she detected an unexpected hint of apology in his manner. "I'd always known that my mother wanted me to marry the daughter of a distant cousin, but it wasn't until after you left that I realized how much she'd resented your presence and how unpleasant she'd made life for you at Cobden Farm. I blame myself that I didn't insist on your having more of a say in how the household was run."

"Our misunderstandings weren't all your mother's fault," Beth said, surprising herself by the admission. "I was strictly a small-town girl from Kentucky, and Cobden Farm was a pretty impressive place, you know. The servants intimidated me and I never really tried to take over from your mother. I guess I haven't much right to complain, if she insisted on doing everything her way."

"I think you're more generous than my mother deserves. After you left she said some things.... Well, anyway, after you left, my mother and I decided that we had different opinions on how important it was for me to find you, and she and I agreed it would be easier if we lived apart."

"You should send her some pictures of Kristin," Beth said impulsively. "As I hear it, most grandmothers are marshmallows once they see a photo of their first grand-child, whatever may have gone on before."

"You're right. She would like to see some pictures." Luke looked at Beth with the hint of a smile darkening his eyes, and she felt an odd little curl of heat began to unwind deep inside her body. She turned away, speaking hurriedly, not giving the feeling a chance to develop.

"I thought your Aunt Maria wanted to retire to Florida," she said.

"She does. She's bought a condo and she plans to live there sometime soon, but when Peppe died we found that we needed each other. I needed somebody to manage Cobden Farm, and Maria badly needed some task that was demanding enough to block out a set of very bad memories. The last few months of Peppe's life were pretty traumatic for her, you know. He was in a great deal of pain, but he was working on an important assignment and he wouldn't take medication until the very end."

"I'm sorry if he suffered," Beth said curtly, all her previous animosity returning in a rush. Maybe it was courageous of Peppe to have refused medication, but his reasons for bearing the pain were hardly noble. Was she supposed to feel sympathy for somebody who'd been so afraid that his criminal cronies might put one over on him that he'd felt compelled to suffer rather than allow his mind to be blurred by pain-killing medication?

Aunt Maria appeared in the doorway just as Beth got out of the car. She had aged visibly in the past two and a half years, but her manner was cheerful and not nearly as nervous as it once had been.

"Beth, how nice to see you. You're looking so well nobody would ever think..." Her voice faded away into a flustered whisper only to rebound again when Luke moved into her line of vision, carrying Kristin. "Oh, my! She's adorable, Beth. You and Luke are lucky to have such a beautiful little girl. Oh, I wish we could have seen her when she was a baby! Come and say hello to your Auntie Maria, honey."

Maria held out her arms, and Kristin went into them quite willingly. Along the way, however, the remnant of her lollipop got stuck inside a fold of her blanket, and she burst into tears.

Although she had never had children of her own, Maria seemed to have an instinctive understanding of what was wrong. She made soothing noises as she unwound the tiny piece of candy from the blanket and showed it to Kristin.

"There, your lollipop's quite safe. We'll take it upstairs and wash it and it'll soon be as good as new. Beth, why don't you come upstairs with me and I'll show you the rooms we've set aside for you and Kristin. That way, Luke and Bill can catch up on their correspondence, and we can get Kristin fed and settled into bed before we all eat dinner. I expect you could use a few minutes peace and quiet yourself."

"I certainly could," Beth said gratefully. "Not to mention a shower. I feel as if I haven't washed for a week."

"It's one of life's minor mysteries," Maria said. "You sit on a plane doing nothing and you end up feeling scruffier and more exhausted than if you'd spent your time digging up the entire garden."

Maria walked up the stairs, patting Kristin soothingly on the back but otherwise ignoring her. Seeing that nobody was paying any attention to her sobs, Kristin stopped crying and began to look around with guarded interest. Luke called out that he'd come up and see her before she went to sleep and Kristin pointedly ignored him. Beth couldn't help feeling a spurt of petty satisfaction when she realized that her daughter's brief truce with Luke was already over.

Aunt Maria stopped outside an oak-paneled door. "I've put you and Kristin in adjoining rooms, and there's a bathroom right across the hall," she said. "Sorry it's not connecting, but that's one of the problems with Cobden Farm. When they renovated it in the fifties, they just didn't put in enough bathrooms."

She threw open the door as she spoke, and Beth literally gasped in astonishment. This room was nothing like the gloomy, antique-filled bedrooms she remembered from her previous stay. Three of the walls were painted pale lemon yellow, and the fourth displayed a colorful floor-to-ceiling mural of teddy bears frolicking in a flower-strewn summer meadow. The soft thick carpet was a rich chocolate brown, and the windows were covered with attractive white shutters. A small bed with a bright yellow quilt nestled in one corner, and a child-size table and chairs occupied the center of the room. A wall of painted shelves held a selection of picture books and simple wooden toys.

"Pretty!" Kristin exclaimed, wriggling excitedly. "See Mama. Look! Pretty!"

"Yes, it is," Beth said. "It's a very pretty room. But I don't understand, Maria. How in the world did Luke manage to get this decorated and furnished so quickly? He only found us yesterday."

"None of this was done yesterday," Maria said, her voice containing a definite hint of reproach. "This room has been ready and waiting for more than two years."

"Two years! But I don't understand—"

"When your brother phoned to say that your baby was born but that he didn't know where you were or anything about the child except that it was healthy, Luke nearly went out of his mind—"

Beth interjected with a whispered "I'm sorry." She flushed, and added, "I'm truly sorry for all the hurt I caused you—"

"You've little reason to apologize to me," Maria said tartly. "I'm not the person you hurt the most."

Beth shifted uncomfortably, all too aware of the irony of her position. She could only defend her actions by explaining exactly why she had run away. Uncle Peppe was dead and could no longer suffer as a result of her revelations, nor could he retaliate. But Luke on the other hand was very much alive. Was she really prepared to put the father of her child in jail? Particularly since, with Peppe dead, he might well have turned over a new leaf and put his corruption behind him. She pressed her hands to her forehead, feeling the start of a pounding relentless headache. Scarcely more than twenty-four hours since Luke had found her, and already all the old moral dilemmas had returned to haunt her. Oh God, now that she was back in Rhode Island, did she have an obligation to tell the D.A. what she had discovered two and a half years ago? She sensed Maria's gaze resting on her burning cheeks, and she forced herself to speak with a calm she was light-years away from feeling.

"Maria, please believe me, I couldn't tell my brother anything more when Kristin was born. There were reasons—good reasons—why I had to behave as I did. There were—are—other people involved, which is why I can't explain precisely why I left Luke."

"Maybe it seemed that way from your perspective, but from Luke's point of view your behavior was pretty hard to take. He knew he was a father, but he didn't even know if his child was a boy or a girl. He drank himself to sleep that first night after your brother called, and he stayed drunk for the rest of the week. When he finally sobered up, he set the best detective agency in the state onto your tail and then drove out to the nearest wallpaper store and selected this paper. He came back and spent three days locked in this room, painting the walls and putting up the paper. He's bought the furniture and the toys gradually over the last two years. It wasn't much of a substitute for watching his baby grow up, but it was all he had."

Beth squeezed her eyes shut, refusing to allow the hot tears to fall. There was no reason for her to feel guilty, she assured herself. Luke was the villain of this piece, not her. However, nothing she could say was going to appease Maria, so she choked back the useless words of apology and silently held out her arms to her daughter. She carried her over to the mural and they examined the tumbling teddy bears together.

Kristin slid down Beth's legs and trotted excitedly back and forth along the wall. She chuckled delightedly as she traced the outline of a particularly fat bear. "My teddy," she said to Beth. "Look, Mama, my teddy!"

Beth wasn't sure whether she wanted to laugh or to cry. Perhaps she wanted to do both. "Yes," she said. "That's just like your teddy bear. Did you see the picture of him eating an ice-cream cone?"

Kristin searched happily for the bear in question, and Maria's expression softened as she watched her great-niece. "Luke finished decorating this room two years ago last September," she said quietly. "None of us thought it would take so long before his child saw what he'd done for her."

Beth could only take so much reproach, particularly when she couldn't defend herself without destroying Maria's memories of her dead husband and incriminating Luke. She drew in a deep breath, forcing herself to produce a bright polite smile.

"Good heavens, time's getting on," she said, glancing at her watch, "and Kristin and I both need a bath. Our luggage seems to have disappeared somewhere between here and the limo. Could you please do me a big favor and track down our suitcases while I see about getting Kristin ready for bed?"

Maria hesitated for no more than a second. "Of course," she said, "and I'll ask the housekeeper if she could make something light for Kristin's dinner. Do you have any suggestions?''

"Some chicken noodle soup would be ideal. It's one of her favorites." Beth smiled again, more genuinely this time. "She's just reached the stage where she won't eat most of the things I think are good for her, and I don't feel strong enough to cope with a full-scale confrontation tonight. I have a horrible suspicion Kristin would win hands down."

Maria's expression was entirely sympathetic. "And every parent I've ever known insists that from age two onward it's all downhill. Their eating habits may get better, but everything else gets worse."

Beth groaned. "Don't tell me about it tonight," she said. "Not after a four-hour plane journey that turned out to last seven hours. I definitely need cosseting."

Maria laughed. "I'll see about that baggage," she said. "Don't forget, Beth, your room's right next door to this one. Towels are all laid out in the bathroom, and you'll find two new toothbrushes in the medicine cabinet."

Kristin ran at lightning speed across the room and tugged at Maria's skirt. "Bye-bye Auntie," she said. She was pleased with her new word and repeated it several times in a singsong chant. "Auntie, Auntie, Auntie." She held up the remnant of lollipop. Its color was almost invisible under a layer of dust and fluff. "For you, Auntie," she added, pressing the soggy white stick into Maria's hand. She smiled again, showing all sixteen of her baby teeth, and folded her hands across her stomach in an unconscious parody of Jessie, her Denver baby-sitter. "Bye-bye Auntie 'Ria. Come back and see us soon."

Maria's eyes misted as she bent down and gathered Kristin into a tight hug. "Oh lord, it's good to have you home," she said softly.

IT RAINED HEAVILY the next morning, the sort of icy penetrating rain typical of New England in November, but the
brightly decorated nursery still seemed full of light and
sunshine. Beth couldn't remember the last time she had
woken up on a Monday morning with nothing to do all day
except enjoy herself. The sensation of freedom and time to
spare was so wonderful that she almost forgot about Luke
and her problems. She lay flat on her stomach on the thick
carpet, building a tower of colored wooden blocks, suppos-
edly for Kristin's benefit. In reality, the blocks came in so
many different shapes, colors and sizes that she was actually enjoying herself. Her building, she decided, looked
like a cross between the ancient Roman Colosseum and the
Houston Astrodome, with a few medieval flying buttresses
thrown in for good measure.

Making strange growling noises as she pulled a wooden
duck around the nursery, Kristen was having almost as much
fun as Beth. Occasionally she would squat and examine the
various angles of her mother's building, before plopping a
block precariously on whatever surface happened to catch
her fancy.

"Mine all red," Kristin said, balancing two yellow blocks
on a corner turret.

"No, those blocks are yellow."

"Lellow?" Kristin repeated. She looked again at her corner. "Mine all red," she said.

"You can call them red if you like, but actually they're
yellow."

Kristin stared at her mother, then in typical two-year-old
fashion, she lost interest in the discussion and pulled her
duck in a wide circle around the tower of blocks, chuckling
gleefully when a section of the outer wall toppled over. Beth
knew it was only a matter of minutes before her daughter
lost interest in the project and rammed her pull toy straight
into the tallest turret. She placed an arch across the second-

level entrance and leaned back on her heels to admire the effect. Maybe she would have time to finish the nifty blue tower she was erecting in the middle of the building....

It was Kristin who alerted Beth to Luke's presence. She suddenly sat down on the floor, hugging her duck tight against her stomach.

"Hello, Man," she said, then scowled and lapsed into an aggressive silence. Not for the first time, it occurred to Beth that her daughter's hostility toward Luke was more than a little odd. Kristin was used to meeting all types of people and, in normal circumstances, was exceptionally easygoing for a toddler. Why did Luke provoke her into such unusual behavior?

"Hello, Kristin. How are you doing this morning?" Luke asked.

Kristin didn't reply, and Beth rose to her feet, nervously pushing a stray golden curl back behind her ear. Luke, immaculately attired in a dark blue three-piece suit, leaned against the doorjamb, the muscles of his broad shoulders taut beneath his tailored jacket. For a moment her heart seemed to alter its rhythm, then she took in the hard assessing stare in his dark eyes, and the heat in her veins cooled as swiftly as it had flared. The brief moment of kinship she had shared with him the day before in the car seemed like a very distant memory.

"Hello, Luke," she said. "We weren't expecting to see you today. The housekeeper told us you were flying to Washington."

"I am," he said. "But I just want to make quite sure that you understand the rules before I leave."

"The rules?"

His shoulders moved in an almost imperceptible shrug. "You'll find them quite simple to follow. You are, of course, entirely free to leave Cobden Farm at any time and for any reason. If you need to shop, the housekeeper has a list of my account numbers at several of the major local stores and you're welcome to charge any purchases to me. If you would like to see a movie or if you need cash for any other reasons, Bill will be happy to advance you some money from petty cash.''

She could feel herself shaking with suppressed rage, and her voice was harsh with humiliation. "If you're trying to be insulting, Luke, you're doing a terrific job, but for your information, I can't be brought into line with the offer of a giant spending spree. I have no intention of spending your money and I certainly would never ask Bill Decker to advance me *anything*. I'd starve first."

"That's entirely up to you," Luke said quietly, but a faint trace of embarrassed color darkened his cheekbones. "It's also up to you whether or not you choose to stay at Cobden Farm. If you decide that you would prefer to leave, Bill will be happy to book you a plane ticket to any destination of your choice. Naturally, the cost of the ticket will be charged to my account."

"Naturally."

He ignored both her interruption and the deliberate irony of her tone. "You probably remember that Cobden Farm is totally surrounded by an electric fence," he said. "However, the police recommended some time ago that we beef up the security system inside the house, and since you left, new sensors have been installed. Without a special encoding card, it's impossible to get in or out through any door or window without setting off an alarm."

She wondered if it really was the police who had recommended increased security or whether Luke had gotten wary of his gangland associates. Peppe's former associates hadn't been men to trifle with. Either way, leaving Cobden Farm was going to be even more difficult than she'd anticipated. She'd expected to be watched. She hadn't expected sophisticated electronic surveillance systems. Beth crossed over to the bed and took Kristin onto her lap, needing to feel the huggable warmth of her daughter's body.

"Are you giving me one of the encoding cards?" she asked, knowing the answer before he replied.

He looked toward her, taking in the protective sweep of her arm around Kristin's shoulders and the scowling wariness of his daughter's expression. His eyes darkened, but he allowed himself no other sign of emotion.

"No," he said finally. "You can't have an encoding card. As I explained, you're free to leave the house whenever you wish—providing you're alone. You won't be allowed to leave with Kristin. You should be warned that everybody here, from the temporary cleaning help all the way up to Aunt Maria, knows that you are never allowed to go out of the house with my daughter unless I'm with you."

Her position in the household would be degrading at best and at worst intolerable, but Beth refused to reveal her dismay. She rose stiffly to her feet, still holding Kristin, and walked over to the window.

"Well, I guess that takes care of everything we have to say to each other," she said.

"Not everything," he said quietly. "But everything that you're ready to hear right now."

His eyes were suddenly bleak, and Beth's stomach clenched tight with an irrational spasm of regret. She wished she didn't feel the need to protect herself by lashing out at Luke, and yet what was the point of wishing that their relationship could be more friendly when she knew she had to leave him? She forced her regrets aside and flashed him an insincere bright smile. "Have a good trip, Congressman, and please don't hurry back on my account."

"I'll be back tomorrow evening." Only the faint flicker of a muscle in his jaw betrayed the fact that he wasn't quite as calm as his voice suggested. He walked across the room and touched Kristin lightly on the arm.

"How was your new bed?" he asked. "I came upstairs to read you a story last night, but you were already asleep."

Kristin pulled the security blanket over her mouth and said nothing.

"I hope you like all those pictures of teddy bears on your wall," Luke continued. "I chose them specially for you as soon as I knew you were born."

Kristin glanced silently at her bed and then at the mural. When she looked up at Luke it was obvious that she had understood exactly what he was asking and was deliberately not answering him.

Beth saw Luke's hands curl in frustration before he shoved them into his trouser pockets. "Kristin, I'm your daddy and I very much want to be your friend. When I come back from my trip, do you think we could spend some time together and learn to be friends?"

Kristin's only answer was to close her eyes and bury her face in Beth's neck. Luke watched them in silence for a moment, then turned abruptly and walked toward the entrance. "Try not to miss me too much while I'm gone," he said and closed the door sharply behind him.

Beth stared at the closed door for a long time until she felt Kristin's tiny fingers clutching at her chin. "What is it, sweetheart?" she asked absently.

"Man is gone," Kristin said. "Look at *me*, don't look at Man."

Beth swiveled around and saw that her daughter's face was crinkled with anxiety. "You is *my* mommy," Kristin said. "Not Man's mommy. Man wants .you to be his mommy."

Beth choked off a gasp of almost hysterical laughter. "Don't worry about it, Kristin. I promise you that Luke doesn't want me to be his mommy."

Kristin wriggled out of her mother's arms and ran over to the tower of blocks. She knelt down and swept her hands through the pile and watched the colored pieces of wood fall into an untidy heap on the dark brown carpet.

"All fall down," she said when the last block had toppled into stillness.

"All fall down," Beth agreed. "Shall we build another tower? An even bigger one?"

Kristin picked up two of the largest blocks and banged them together, her forehead wrinkled in concentration. "Man is your daddy?" she asked.

"No, Luke isn't my daddy, he's my husband." Beth clasped her hands tightly in front of her, knowing that Kristin wouldn't understand the word husband and not at all sure why she felt compelled to explain any further. "Luke is your daddy, Kristin. He's your father."

Kristin threw the blocks she was holding onto the floor and picked up her stuffed yellow bear. "Teddy is my daddy," she said in a tone that brooked no argument.

She turned her back on Beth and walked determinedly toward the shelf of toys. She found a toy drum and beat on it experimentally a couple of times. "Teddy is my daddy," she muttered, banging the drum more and more loudly. Soon the fascination of the rhythm absorbed all of her attention. She walked around the room, pounding the drum and laughing with uninhibited pleasure at the amount of noise she could produce. Luke was clearly forgotten.

Beth envied her daughter. She knew that, unfortunately, it would take something more powerful than a toy drum to obliterate Luke from her own thoughts.

CHAPTER SEVEN

THE RAIN STOPPED on Monday night, and by lunchtime on Tuesday the sun had dried up the worst of the mud puddles. Aunt Maria, who seemed as proud of the clear skies as if she personally were responsible for the improved weather, volunteered to take Kristin to the local library, where a group of puppeteers was scheduled to put on a performance especially for preschoolers.

Kristin was enthusiastic at the prospect of an outing, and Beth took advantage of her free afternoon to borrow one of the estate cars and drive into Providence. She told herself that she had no particular destination in mind, but the third time she circled the building that housed the D.A.'s office, she gave up trying to deceive herself. She turned into the crowded parking lot and sat inside her car nursing the keys for several minutes. Why was she doing this? What was she hoping to prove? She was inside the elevator, pressing the button for the D.A.'s office on the seventh floor, when she finally acknowledged the truth. She wanted a miracle, she realized. She wanted the D.A. to tell her that the Timberline Construction Company had never cheated the state of Rhode Island out of millions of dollars. She wanted the D.A. to tell her that Luke was innocent of all wrongdoing.

Beth felt her mouth twist into a hard self-mocking smile. She surely had to be one of the world's slowest learners where her husband was concerned. Why, despite all the evidence to the contrary, did she still cherish the ridiculous hope that somehow Luke had been innocent? Why did she still find herself thinking that he really cared about his constituents, that his honesty and hard work were genuine characteristics and not merely a clever facade?

Richard Descartes, the assistant prosecutor and one of her former colleagues, happened to be talking to the receptionist when Beth entered the D.A.'s outer office. He welcomed her with a little exclamation of astonishment and a hearty clap on the back.

"We heard you were studying overseas," he said. "Working with one of the U.N. agencies. How does it feel to be back in Rhode Island?"

So that was the story Luke had invented to explain her sudden absence, Beth thought. She decided there was no point in correcting Richard's misunderstanding. "I've only been back here a couple of days, so I'm not quite sure," she replied truthfully enough. "But my daughter seems to think it's a great place. She loves the ocean, even when it's raining."

"My kids are the same. I swear they'd swim in December if we turned them loose. Look, why don't you come into my office and I'll see if I can rustle up a decent cup of coffee. I'll fill you in on what's been happening here, and you can tell me all about that workaholic husband of yours. We never see him anymore. Is he really going to make a bid for the Senate next year?"

Beth followed Richard into his office and cleared a shopping bag and a pile of legal briefs off the only available chair. She smiled wryly as she sat down, glad of an excuse to avoid answering his question. "Some things never change, Richard. I don't know how in the world you ever find anything you're looking for."

He grinned, not a whit embarrassed. "My filing system's failsafe. It's just that I'm the only person who knows how to work it."

Beth tipped her chair back. "So how's crime in the state of Rhode Island?" she asked with an attempt at casualness that sounded totally phony to her tense ears.

Fortunately Richard was preoccupied with pouring out two cups of coffee and didn't seem to hear the quiver in her voice. He handed her a steaming mug of coffee, then perched on the edge of his desk and began to give her a quick rundown of some of the more interesting cases currently under investigation. He also passed on a few pieces of harmless office gossip. The former D.A. had been promoted to a federal judgeship, an honor Richard seemed to think was well deserved. The new D.A. was a decent guy, but in Richard's opinion, he lacked his predecessor's skill in attacking the bastions of organized crime.

Beth cradled her mug of coffee and took a long slow sip. "I read some interesting stuff about the Timberline Construction Company," she said. "This office brought in a whole slew of indictments about eighteen months ago. It isn't often that a local D.A. can bring in indictments that hit the national press."

"Yes, our office sure did a good job on that one," Richard said proudly. "Actually, those indictments came down about two years ago, not long after you left us in fact. The Timberline case was the last one the D.A. handled before he moved to the federal court. He managed to get convictions against virtually every senior officer in that whole damn company. Those bastards had bilked the state of close to six million dollars, and what's more, they'd built substandard bridges in the process. We're lucky we managed to put them away and get access to their records before they caused a major tragedy. They were paying off inspectors in the Building Department and the State Highway Department, of course. God knows how many inspectors were involved, but we managed to get convictions against three of them. We even managed to put a couple of federal inspectors

away, including one guy working right at the top level of the
Department of Transportation in Washington. He got five
years, the crooked swine. We could never prove it, but we
think he'd been taking payments from Building
Departments all over the country. We know for sure that
Timberline was planning to close down its operations here
and move in on Pennsylvania, and some guy in Washington was preparing to grease the move."

Beth felt sweat converge in an icy trickle across the back
of her neck. Uncle Peppe had obviously died just in time,
and how Luke had escaped the D.A.'s net she would never
know. Was it possible that the D.A. had been persuaded to
turn a blind eye in return for his judgeship? Beth quickly
rejected the idea. Surely even the powerful Caine family
would have been unable to secure a judgeship for someone
who didn't deserve it.

Somehow she managed to voice a few suitably casual
compliments before steering the conversation back onto less
dangerous ground. She didn't want Richard Descartes to
remember too many details about their talk, so she spent
another half hour with him, walking around the various
offices and renewing her acquaintance with several of her
former colleagues.

"Melissa Petersen's leaving next month," Richard re-
marked as he escorted her to the elevator. "Her husband's
been transferred to California. You should give some
thought to applying for her position. We'd all like to have
you back. We made a good team."

Beth stretched her mouth into a smile. "Thanks for the
invitation, but I'm not quite sure what my plans are right
now."

Richard laughed. "Ah-ha! You've been very discreet so
far, Beth, but now I'm certain Luke's running for senator!
You're going to act as legal advisor to his campaign, right?"

Beth's jaw muscles ached from holding her smile in place. "Nothing's decided yet," she said.

Richard held open the elevator door. "He'll win easily, you know. He's intelligent, hardworking and has a broad enough appeal that the voters know he won't be tied into anybody's pocket. I'm glad he's going to run. We need somebody with his sort of integrity."

Integrity! Dear God, if only he knew the truth. Beth's smile finally gave out. "It's been great seeing you, Richard, but I really have to go. My daughter will think I've abandoned her." She stepped into the elevator and didn't even wait for the doors to close fully before she leaned against the wall, clutching her stomach to prevent the waves of nausea from overwhelming her. She'd wanted to discover the truth and now she had. The truth was that the Timberline Construction Company was every bit as corrupt as she'd suspected. And as far as she could see, the only people connected with the company who'd avoided prosecution were Peppe Bellini and Luke Caine.

LUKE ARRIVED BACK FROM WASHINGTON around seven o'clock. Much to her chagrin, Beth met him in the upstairs hallway when she was coming out of the bathroom, her wet hair bundled up in a towel and her skin still glowing and damp from the shower. She would have slipped into her bedroom without speaking to him, but he covered her hand and prevented her from opening the door.

"Beth, would you go out for dinner with me tonight? There are some things I think we need to discuss. Urgently."

She felt flustered when she looked up at him, which must have been the reason for the sudden flare of heat that suffused her body. He was wearing yet another of his five-hundred-dollar business suits, but he had taken off the jacket and carried it slung casually over one shoulder. He had also loosened the knot of his tie and unfastened the top button of his shirt, so she could see a few inches of tanned skin between the slashes of pristine cotton broadcloth. If he had unfastened one more button, she would have been able to see the hair that grew in a dark narrow vee from the top of his chest down to below his waistline. Sometimes when she had wanted to arouse him she had run her tongue slowly down that soft line of hair while her hands traced tiny provocative circles around— Abruptly Beth cut off the too-vivid memories, horrified at where her thoughts were leading her. She folded her arms tightly around her body in an attempt to subdue the sensations rioting deep inside her.

"I think we probably ought to hold all of our conversations in a lawyer's office," she said tautly. "Not over a dinner table. I can't think of anything we need to discuss privately."

"Can't you, Beth? Do you really want our daughter's fate to be decided by some overworked judge who knows nothing about Kristin except what our respective lawyers choose to tell him?"

"No, of course not, but—"

"God knows it's been difficult for me to accept what you did, but I trust you enough to believe that you truly want what's best for our child. Can't you believe the same about me? Wouldn't it be better for Kristin if we discussed our ideas about custody rationally, just the two of us?"

"Maybe. I'm not sure...."

He took the end of the towel and patted a droplet of water that had started to trickle between her breasts. "Have dinner with me tonight," he repeated, his voice oddly husky.

She made a soft helpless whisper of protest deep in her throat, but somehow the words that finally emerged were words of acceptance, not of denial. Later, when she was alone in her room, she tried to rationalize what she had done, but she was basically too honest for self-deception.

The uncomfortable truth was that she had agreed to go out with Luke because she wanted to be with him and for no other reason. The information she had gleaned today in the D.A.'s office, damning as it was, had made no real difference to her still-existing state of infatuation.

Choosing what she would wear required all of thirty seconds. Her budget over the past two years hadn't stretched to much more than durable pants teamed with wash-and-wear tops. She possessed only one outfit that had any pretensions to elegance, a practical heather-gray tweed skirt and matching wool jacket, bought for job interviews the previous fall. Ironically enough she had discovered that the shadier and more dubious the employer, the more likely he was to hire people who looked respectable. She was convinced it was the sober gray suit that had won her employment first in an Omaha bar and then in a Kansas City all-night disco.

She had no slinky silk blouse or elegant little designer scarf to pretty up her outfit. She shrugged resignedly as she buttoned up her white polyester shirt and slipped on the unlined woolen jacket. Kristin grew so fast that even for job interviews Beth's budget hadn't stretched to more than the superficial appearance of elegance.

She smoothed on some lip gloss and darkened her lashes with mascara, not even bothering to look into the full-length mirror to check her appearance. Perhaps it was just as well she didn't possess any exotic designer dresses, Beth reflected. Despite everything, she was probably crazy enough where Luke was concerned to find herself dressing up to please him.

She slipped into Kristin's room to kiss her good-night. A dim night-light provided the only illumination, but Beth could see that her daughter was already asleep. She lay flat on her back, snoring softly, her arms flung wide and her teddy bear resting precariously on her chest. Kristin wasn't alone. Luke stood unmoving at the side of her bed, his hands clasped convulsively around the low bed rail. Beth knew instinctively, beyond any possibility of doubt, that he longed to reach out and touch his daughter, but that for some reason he was afraid to do so.

She walked quietly across the room, making no sound on the thick carpet. She was almost at Kristin's bedside before Luke realized he was no longer alone. He immediately moved away from the bed, angling himself so that his features remained hidden.

Beth didn't speak to him. She removed the teddy bear to a distant spot on the pillow and quickly rolled Kristin over onto her side. The snoring ceased immediately and Kristin's eyes flickered open. Her mouth wobbled into a smile. "Mama," she said in a pleased voice, before she drifted off again into deep peaceful sleep.

Beth dropped a swift kiss onto her daughter's pink cheek, then nuzzled her neck for a moment before straightening and looking at Luke. "I'm ready to leave for dinner anytime you are," she said quietly.

He kept his face averted, and his hand moved briefly across his eyes. Disbelieving, Beth had the impression that he was wiping away tears. For a long moment he didn't answer her, and when he finally spoke his voice was raw with suppressed emotion. "I'm her father, for God's sake, but I was afraid to touch her." He gave a ghost of a laugh. "It's ironic, isn't it? I thought she'd be frightened if she woke up and saw me."

Beth spoke without stopping to weigh her words. "Don't worry so much, Luke. She'll soon get used to you."

"Sure. And in a couple more years, she may even stop calling me Man." He finally swung around, gesturing impatiently, and Beth stole a covert glance at him. She must have been imagining things, she decided, for she could detect no trace of tears.

"What the hell," Luke said. "We'd better be going. I've made reservations for eight o'clock and it's almost that time already."

"I'm sure any restaurant owner in this state would be delighted to save a table for the famous Congressman Luke Caine."

He looked at her searchingly, not bothering to conceal his genuine puzzlement. "Beth, would you please explain something to me? Why do you hate me so much?"

Because I daren't risk feeling anything else for you. The words sprang unbidden into her mind and she tossed them out as quickly as they had come. "Shouldn't we be on our way?" she said, walking determinedly toward the door. "As a matter of fact I skipped lunch today and I'm feeling hungry."

Luke didn't press for a more appropriate answer to his question. Perhaps he had never expected one. He left word with Aunt Maria about where they were going and politely escorted Beth to the front door. A Cadillac Sedan de-Ville waited for them in the driveway—inconspicuous, dark and discreetly luxurious. Congressman Caine never missed a trick, Beth reflected cynically. He had too much savvy to offend his constituents by driving a flashy foreign import.

Luke carried most of the burden of the conversation on the way to the restaurant. He kept their discussion well away from any personal topics, mentioning some of the more controversial legislation pending in Congress. When they were first married he had been Chairman of the House Select Committee on Organized Crime, but he had been promoted recently to the more prestigious House Finance Committee. Beth had never doubted that he took some aspects of his work in Congress very seriously, and he seemed genuinely interested as he asked her opinion of various schemes for reducing the federal budget deficit. It was his evident dedication to his work that made her dilemma so difficult, she thought with a touch of despair. She had no doubt at all that in many ways Luke was an outstanding member of the House of Representatives.

The restaurant was pleasantly low-key, serving traditional American fare of steaks and seafood, sparked up with a few elegant French touches. Luke had obviously made up his mind to put controversy aside, and he was a delightful dinner companion: charming, witty and devastatingly entertaining. Beth fought constantly against drifting into a dangerously beguiling time warp. It would have been so easy to imagine that they were back in Washington, back in the early days of their relationship when merely to be near Luke was to send her senses into a tailspin of heightened awareness. It would have been so easy to imagine they were back in those wonderful days when every minute spent in his company seemed to provide fresh proof that his mind and soul marched in absolute harmony with her own. It was so perilously easy to forget all that had happened in the past three years—especially when he smiled at her with just that touch of tender rueful wistfulness.

Beth clutched her glass of California burgundy and drank deeply. "You said you wanted to talk about a custody agreement for Kristin," she said abruptly. "I thought that was why we came here."

"It was one of the reasons," he agreed. He took a forkful of baked potato, then put the fork down on his plate without eating. "Beth, we're rational adults and I'm sure we both want to do what's right for Kristin. You've probably read all the same child-care manuals I have, so we know that young children thrive better if they're brought up in a home where there are two loving parents."

"Unfortunately in practice we can't always follow the theory."

"I know. But in our case, I think we could come pretty close to providing Kristin with an ideal environment, at least for the next few years."

"What are you suggesting?"

"I'm suggesting that in some ways we're luckier than a lot of parents who discover they don't want to live together anymore. Cobden Farm is very large and I travel a great deal. I assume that eventually you'd like to resume your career as a lawyer, which means you'll be spending a fair amount of time away from the house. In the circumstances, it seems to me that we could both continue to live at Cobden Farm almost indefinitely without ever really seeing one another, and the benefits to Kristin would be enormous."

Luke pushed his plate away, at least half of his dinner still uneaten. "I'm not a fool, Beth. I realize you're planning either to fight me for custody through the courts or else to steal Kristin away as soon as you get the opportunity. But there isn't much point in running, you know. Now that I've found her, I'll never let my daughter disappear from my life again. Wherever you go with her, I'll track you down eventually. Is that really what you want for our daughter? A lifetime of fighting and snatching and running?" He reached out and, taking her hand, held it between his long tanned fingers. Her body immediately became suffused with a treacherous languorous heat. "It doesn't have to be that way," he said huskily. His thumbs traced a delicate caressing pattern across her knuckles. "Whatever our feelings for each other, Beth, I think we can do better for our child than that."

His eyes were so damned *honest*, she thought painfully. She drew in a shaky breath and forced herself to remove her hand from his clasp. It was so unfair that he should have the power to make her question all her hard-won decisions, she thought. She visualized a future in which she was condemned to endless glimpses of Luke, with no possibility of intimacy or even of friendship, and her entire body shuddered in revulsion. Better, far better, to spend her life on the run than to endure the torment of being so near him, constantly tempted to bury the memory of what he had done in the wild consuming pleasures of his lovemaking.

Once, a lifetime ago, she would have been naive enough to reject his plan openly. Now, after two years on the run, she was a much wiser woman. Luke was wary of her intentions, and if she was going to escape from him again, it would require very careful planning. Her first requirement was to do everything in her power to lull his suspicions.

"Your plan sounds reasonable," she said, pretending to consider his suggestion. "And I can see the advantages from Kristin's point of view. But I'm not sure that any house is big enough to hold two people who really dislike each other."

"Do we dislike each other?" he asked quietly. "Somehow, despite everything, I've never quite managed to convince myself that we do."

Beth closed her eyes, clenching her fists and wrapping her resistance around herself like a shield. She couldn't afford the luxury of considering what the true answer to Luke's question might be. "I think we would find it... uncomfortable to live in the same house," she said finally, her voice flat from the effort of suppressing her emotions.

"Maybe, but what are our alternatives? Are you really prepared to take your chances on a full-blown custody battle? Are you a hundred percent certain you'd win? I'll be honest with you, Beth. I have no idea how a judge would decide between us, and that's why I made this suggestion."

"I'm not at all sure I'd win custody of Kristin," she admitted. "Custody decisions don't always go in favor of the mother anymore, and you can obviously provide Kristin with material advantages that would be impossible for me.''

"Then why won't you consider staying on at Cobden Farm? What have you got to lose?''

Only my integrity, my sanity and my self-respect, Beth thought with a flash of black humor. She decided that her opposition to his plan had lasted long enough to be convincing, and she settled back in her chair, lifting her wine glass and draining the final few drops.

"I guess Cobden Farm is a pretty big place. We ought to be able to keep out of each other's way. And you're right, I am planning to go back to work.''

"Any idea where?''

Some imp of mischief caused her to probe for a break in his impeccable facade. "Yes, as a matter of fact, I went to the D.A.'s office today. You know, my old stomping ground in Providence.''

"Oh yes. Did you meet the new D.A.?''

"Only briefly. But I spent quite a lot of time with some of my former colleagues.'' She studied his face for any hint of a reaction, but his expression revealed nothing more than polite interest. Nevertheless, she ploughed doggedly on. "Do you remember Richard Descartes? Well, he told me that there's a vacancy for an assistant prosecutor coming up shortly. I was thinking about taking it.''

"If that's what you want, I'm all in favor," Luke said. His smile seemed warm, encouraging—and completely sincere. "I'm sure Aunt Maria would love to act as baby-sitter, and the D.A.'s office could use your professional skills. This new D.A. doesn't have half the street smarts of the old one. He needs a good team around him if he's ever going to halt the growth of organized crime in this state.''

Beth's fingers closed so tightly around the stem of her wine glass that she realized she was in danger of breaking it. She had no idea why she kept devising these useless little

tests; she ought to have learned by now that Luke never revealed the slightest hint of guilt or uneasiness. She glanced
at her watch and deliberately changed the subject. "It's
getting late, and Kristin always wakes up at the crack of
dawn. If you're planning to order dessert, Luke, maybe we
should try to attract the waiter's attention."

"I can recommend the raspberry ice cream," he said.
"But speaking personally, I've sworn off desserts. My
trousers have been getting tighter and tighter over the past
few weeks, and I've finally decided I have to stop blaming
the dry cleaners." He grinned. "Every so often a man has
to face up to harsh reality, and I've finally admitted that my
pants aren't shrinking—my stomach is expanding."

"I hadn't noticed any change," Beth said.

Luke's dark eyes gleamed. "No? But then you haven't
seen me recently without my clothes."

An image of Luke's sleek muscular body flashed into her
mind, unbidden and totally unwanted. She remembered the
nights she had lain next to him in the huge old-fashioned
bed, their bodies taut with the tension of their lovemaking,
their mouths clinging together with aching desperate hunger. Desire flared within her, heating her blood and blur-
ring her mind. She closed her eyes, shutting out the
memories, then crumpled her napkin into a tight ball and
tossed it onto the table. "I'll skip dessert, thanks all the
same. I guess I'm ready to leave, unless you want coffee."

"No, I don't want coffee." Luke's eyes were heavy-
lidded, his voice husky. Beth wondered how he could make
such a simple statement seem so loaded with sensual meaning.

It occurred to her belatedly that perhaps she was imagining the sexual tension that thickened the air between them.
She had spent the past two years in a state of celibacy, but
her husband was unlikely to have been similarly deprived.
Naive as she'd been when she first met Luke, Beth had in-

stantly recognized that good looks and charm were only a small part of his appeal. The dynamic, magnetic sense of power he projected had exerted a potent appeal even to an inexperienced, small-town girl like her. To the sophisticated women on the Washington cocktail circuit, where power was the ultimate aphrodisiac, Luke would always be irresistible. Beth found the thought of her husband making love to another woman unbearably hurtful, and she rose hurriedly to her feet.

He didn't attempt to detain her. He joined her a few minutes later and escorted her silently to the car. "Tell me about Kristin," he said, as he drove out of the half-empty parking lot. "How do you think she's settling in? She seems to get on well with Aunt Maria."

Beth agreed and told him how much Kristin liked her new bedroom. She never found any difficulty in talking about her daughter, but she discovered that there was a special pleasure in recounting anecdotes to somebody who cared as vitally and as deeply for Kristin as she did. She talked nonstop during the journey home, realizing as the words poured out of her just how many details of Kristin's babyhood had been bottled up inside her, waiting to be shared.

Luke parked the car in one of the garages, and they walked slowly across the deserted courtyard to the patio door. Aunt Maria always went to bed early, and the house was silent, the hallways lit only by the dim glow of low-wattage bulbs left on all night. By unspoken agreement, they went upstairs to Kristin's room.

Her door was ajar, allowing a beam of light to enter from the corridor. She lay on her stomach, her security blanket pressed against her nose and her curls spread out in a tumbled mass against the pillow. She didn't stir when Beth smoothed her hair out of her eyes and tucked her shoulders under the bright yellow quilt. Luke said nothing, watching them in silence until Beth moved away from the bed, then he leaned down and kissed his daughter.

"Kissing her while she's asleep is okay," he said, as they came out of Kristin's room into the corridor. "But I'm looking forward to the day she's awake and she lets me kiss her. That, and the day she stops calling me Man."

"Don't take her attitude too personally," Beth said, opening the door to her bedroom. "We moved a lot, and in some ways she's learned to adapt easily to new people. But she's been brought up in a strictly female world. Until you came along, there weren't really any men in her life at all."

"Weren't there?" Luke asked softly. He streched out his arm, barring the entrance to her bedroom. "You know something? I think that's probably the best news I've heard in a long time."

Beth looked at him and he looked at her. Then they both hastily looked away. Neither of them dared to glance into her room, where the bed suddenly seemed to stand conspicuously empty—and conspicuously inviting. Beth cleared her throat.

"Well, good night, Luke . . ."

"Don't go," he said. Slowly, deliberately, he raised his hands and cupped her face, brushing his thumbs lightly across her cheekbone. "I've missed you," he said simply.

Beth tried to ignore the fact that her legs no longer seemed to have the power to support her body. She stiffened her spine, refusing to succumb to the overwhelming urge to rest her head on Luke's broad inviting shoulders. She refused to acknowledge the ripples of sensation spreading out from his thumbs and radiating all the way down to her toes.

"Well, anyway, Luke, thanks for a delicious dinner," she said, wondering if her bright chirpy voice sounded as absurd to him as it did to her. She smiled nervously. "It's been a while since I ate such good steak."

"Believe me, it was my pleasure," he said, laughter and tenderness softening the formal politeness of his words. His head bent inexorably toward her mouth. "It's always my pleasure to be with you," he whispered, his lips only a breath away from hers.

Her heart stopped beating, then seemed to race at three times its normal speed. "Gosh, it's past midnight," she said, glancing desperately at her wristwatch. She was aware that the situation had somehow slipped entirely out of her control, but she had no idea how she could retrieve it. "Luke, it's late. I think we should go to bed."

He gave a laugh that was almost a groan. "So do I," he murmured. "In fact, I've been thinking about little else for the last three days."

Beth's legs completed their treacherous transformation into liquid rubber and refused categorically to continue supporting her. She swayed into Luke's arms and he pulled her urgently against his thighs.

"Beth, my love, it's been so damn long! Sometimes late at night I lie in bed and wonder if it really is possible to die from wanting someone."

His voice was a rough whisper that echoed deep inside her soul. It awakened passions she had spent two long lonely years learning to subdue. Her eyes drifted shut as he closed the infinitesimal gap between their mouths and parted her lips with slow persuasive strokes of his tongue. A shudder ripped through his entire body when she finally surrendered her mouth to the domination of his kiss. His skilled masterful caresses appeased her hunger and yet somehow left her craving more, and she moved her hips against his in automatic unconscious invitation. She ought to have been horrified at the sensations he was arousing in her, but instead she rejoiced in the knowledge that she still retained the power to turn his overwhelming strength into a trembling weakness.

His weakness was strictly relative, however. He bent suddenly and picked her up, carried her effortlessly down the hall and shouldered open the door that led to his bedroom. The room, Beth realized, that had once been theirs. The room where Kristin had been conceived.

He tossed back the covers of the bed and lowered her onto the pillows, his hands stroking restlessly through her tumbled curls. "Oh God!" he said. "Beth, if this is a dream, then please don't wake me."

The husky timbre of his voice drugged her mind at the same time as it heightened her physical responses. His body was hard against her softness, and the heat of his breath teased her skin. She was alive with the need for him, aching for the supreme pleasure of joining her body to his.

She tried vainly to marshal some semblance of rational thought. She reminded herself that Luke had always used sex as a weapon to deflect her questions. She reminded herself of all the reasons she had to mistrust him, but reason seemed elusive now and the heat of his kisses so very real. His passion reached out to her, trapping her in its path like the heat traveling in advance of a forest fire. Her mind might hesitate on the brink of surrender to the final conflagration, but her body had already welcomed the flames.

Luke lifted his head from their kiss. "You're wearing far too many clothes," he murmured.

"That's easily cured," she said, and in a fit of ultimate, self-destructive insanity, reached up and unfastened the buttons at the neck of her blouse. Her gaze locked with Luke's, and she watched sweat bead across his forehead as she slowly undid the row of buttons. When the last one was unfastened, she reached up and grasped his shoulders, pulling him down onto the pillows.

"You make me crazy," he said, his voice thick, almost harsh. He bent his head to one of her breasts and sucked the tip through the thin lace covering of her bra. He wrapped one hand around her wrists and gently raised her arms over her head. Then with his other hand he released the catch of her bra and she felt the hot moistness of his mouth closing over her nipple. Desire uncoiled in the pit of her stomach, fierce and unrelenting in its demands. She arched her body upward, pressing her breast deeper into his mouth. His arms slid down and tightened around her hips, thrusting her against him in such a way that there was no mistaking his intent or the extent of his arousal.

She moaned weakly, turning her head in a belated meaningless gesture of denial.

"No..." she muttered. "No, Luke, please, I don't want this...." But it was no more than a token protest and they both knew it—a final sop to her conscience, a last flickering moment of rationality in the heated darkness of their passion. Her body had long since told him everything he needed to know about how willing she was to submit to his caresses.

He undid the catch at the waistband of her skirt, and she gasped with pleasure as she felt her flesh released from the confinement of the woolen cloth. Luke's breath whispered over her sensitive skin, and she shivered beneath the hot touch of his tongue. From somewhere far, far away she heard the sound of banging hammers, and with a distant part of her brain she wondered why carpenters were working at this late hour of the night. Then Luke kissed her again, and soon there was no room inside her head for logical thinking.

But the banging refused to stop. Instead it grew louder, and Luke finally lifted his head. Reluctantly they registered the fact that the noise wasn't a distant hammering, but rather someone knocking on the bedroom door. Luke muttered a low curse, then rolled away from her and got to his feet in a single fluid movement.

She lay rigid on the bed too dazed to move, feeling the embers of desire circulate like a drug in her veins. She watched as Luke opened the door and was relieved when he held it at such an angle that the bed was invisible to whoever was knocking. With a small smothered sound, she twisted onto her stomach, fighting for control of her own body.

"I'm sorry to bother you, Luke." Aunt Maria's flustered voice carried clearly into the bedroom. "I know you switch off your phone extension when you don't want to be disturbed, and I wouldn't have troubled you except in an emergency. The ambassador is calling from El Gabon in South America. It's something about a group of teenagers, all of them from Rhode Island, who've been caught in the middle of a local revolution."

"You were quite right to wake me," Luke said. "Thanks for passing on the message, Maria. I'll pick up the call in here."

He closed the door and strode immediately to his desk. "Luke Caine speaking," he said, picking up the phone. "Sorry to have kept you waiting, Ambassador. How can I help you?"

Beth got off the bed and stood up as quietly as she could. She buttoned her blouse with fingers that shook visibly. Luke watched her, his eyes dark and totally unreadable, but his attention was clearly focused on the information he was receiving from the ambassador. Sorry as she felt for the teenagers trapped by a battle that was none of their making, Beth couldn't help feeling that the Gabonese revolutionaries, whoever they were, had unwittingly saved her from making a disastrous mistake.

"Even if I can reach everybody, it'll take me a minimum of ten phone calls to get all the information you need," she heard Luke say. "Will you call me again in an hour? I assume your phone lines are protected against wiretaps. Mine aren't."

Beth slipped out of the room without speaking and walked down the hallway toward her own room and bed. She knew Luke wouldn't approach her again that night. In fact she had no doubt that his personal life would be put on hold indefinitely if the ambassador indicated that there was any way in which Luke could be of help in freeing the young Rhode Islanders.

For at least the hundredth time Beth wondered how somebody who had sold out his fellow citizens to a gaggle of crooks and con men could show such unfailing dedication in so many other areas of his job.

Morning arrived long before she had produced any satisfactory answer to her question. As she dressed Kristin for the day Beth realized that she knew only one fact about herself and Luke with any certainty. Last night's lovemaking had not been a temporary aberration on her part. Unfortunately, for whatever combination of reasons, she was so susceptible to Luke's physical attractions that she couldn't rely on resisting him. If she stayed here, sooner or later she would violate every principle she valued and end up in his bed. And once they made love again, she wasn't at all sure that she would have the strength to leave him.

Even now her body ached with the frustration of the previous night's unconsummated lovemaking, and she was afraid that if she found herself alone with Luke, she wouldn't have the willpower to resist him. The temptation to surrender to the sensual joy of his possession was almost overwhelming. Her conscience might be full of moral doubts, but her body had no doubts at all. It was telling her—urgently and specifically—exactly what it wanted. And her body wanted Luke.

There was only one logical solution to her dilemma, Beth concluded. She had to get away. For her own sake, every bit as much as for Kristin's, she had to escape from Cobden Farm before her body betrayed her.

CHAPTER EIGHT

TWO DAYS OF INTENSIVE, high-level negotiations were required before the new government of El Gabon allowed an American military plane to land and evacuate the twelve Rhode Island college students and their accompanying professors. The group had been studying the basic principles of archaeological research as it applied to the early American Indian. Isolated in a village halfway up a mountain, they had been blissfully unaware of the deteriorating national situation until they found themselves sitting in the middle of two opposing factions, each bound and determined to blow up the village.

When the students were safely home, Luke appeared on national television and delivered a brief lecture on the obligation of Americans to be well informed of the political conditions in foreign countries before establishing themselves in the illusory safety of a distant mountainside.

Beth, watching the program in the kitchen with the housekeeper while Kristin ate her dinner, thought that few politicians had Luke's almost magical skill for delivering stern lessons in a manner that remained relaxed and entirely good-humored. Beth cut the remainder of her daughter's chicken into small bite-size pieces as the interviewer continued his questions.

"I understand, Congressman, that you personally negotiated the deal that persuaded the revolutionary armies to allow the American military transport plane to land."

Beth saw the faint, almost indiscernible frown that momentarily tightened Luke's features. "The safe conduct for our citizens was a cooperative effort by several people and many government agencies," he replied. "Our ambassador in El Gabon acted with tremendous courage in setting the first stage of the negotiations in motion."

"Nevertheless, Congressman, I understand from at least three sources that it was your personal friendship with General Miguel that finally persuaded him to allow our plane to land in territory his army is holding."

"Miguel and I were in law school together here in the States," Luke conceded tersely. "But Miguel is a highly intelligent, well-educated man. There's no reason to suppose he would have allowed American citizens, particularly young college students, to become victims of the internal strife that, sadly enough, is devastating his country."

Kristin finished her last mouthful of chicken and stared with unusual concentration at the television. Her face suddenly broke into a smile. "My Man," she said pointing at the screen. "Look, Mama, he is our Man. My Man is nice."

Beth's stomach felt hollow. "Yes," she said, "that's your daddy."

Evelyn, the housekeeper, brought Kristin a half-peeled banana and chucked her lovingly under the chin. "Aren't you surprised, seeing your daddy on television? And he's certainly a man for any little girl to be proud of. Can you say daddy yet? That's not a hard word, is it? Say daddy, Kristin."

Kristin didn't answer the housekeeper because she was staring at the television. "Man is all gone," she announced finally and took a large bite of banana. Beth and Evelyn glanced up simultaneously to find that Luke's image had been replaced by an advertisement for the newest and "best" in diet soft drinks.

Two seconds later, Bill Decker pushed open the kitchen door and stormed over to the fridge. "Sorry for intruding," he said with a quick nod toward Beth, "but we need a couple of cold beers in the office. Luke's campaign manager is over here discussing strategy, and he's about to have an apoplexy."

Evelyn grunted. "That's nothing new. He's only happy when he's inventing some new crisis."

"What's his problem this time?" Beth asked, somewhat amused by the contrast between Bill Decker's agitation and the housekeeper's unruffled calm.

"Good grief, didn't either of you hear the news? That damned newscaster got Luke to admit that he's known General Miguel for years. Before you know it, the right wing press will be saying Luke's sympathetic to the revolutionaries."

Beth felt as if somebody had landed a hard blow to her ribs.

"Would that be so bad?" she asked.

Bill snorted. "Depends on what you want to do with your life. It's about as bad as it can get if you want to be elected senator. The citizens of this state like nice, solid, middle-of-the-road people to represent them, not way-out kooks from the left or the right of the political spectrum."

So that was why Luke had frowned at the question about General Miguel, Beth reflected. And to think she had naively assumed he was modest and upset about having his role in the rescue operation thrown into too much prominence! Good lord, would she never learn to see Luke as he really was and not as she wanted to imagine him?

"Luke doesn't necessarily approve of General Miguel's politics just because they went to the same law school," she said, feeling the need to make some response to Bill's revelations.

"You and I both know that. Try telling it to those right wing reporters who are out to get him." Bill popped the top on one of the beer cans and hurried toward the door. "I'd better get back to Gerry and see if this will calm him down. He told Luke not to get involved with this whole horrible situation, and now he's breathing fire and brimstone about all the potential repercussions. Sometimes you can't afford to do people a good turn. God knows, Luke ought to have learned that by now. He's the world's original bleeding heart."

Beth watched Bill Decker's departure with troubled eyes. The housekeeper ambled over to Kristin's high chair and picked up the banana skin. "You don't want to pay any attention to Bill and those campaign men he's hired," she said to Beth. Her smile was comfortable, almost placid. "Thank the good Lord that Mr. Caine's got more sense than to listen to them most of the time. He knows what's right even if they don't." She wiped Kristin's sticky fingers with a damp paper towel. "Mr. Caine's going to romp into the Senate next year, you'll see. Bill Decker and that campaign manager, they just like to invent problems."

"Some people enjoy worrying," Beth agreed. The housekeeper was absolutely right, she thought, feeling a sudden spurt of irritation with herself. Bill Decker had always prided himself on seeing the worst of any situation, but there was no reason she should share Bill's cynicism. Her instincts had suggested that Luke frowned because the television interviewer gave him too much credit for rescuing the students from El Gabon. Why couldn't she trust her instincts? The fact that Luke once accepted a bribe didn't necessarily mean that *every* action he took had tainted motives.

The housekeeper finished stowing mugs in the dishwasher. She pressed the controls and straightened up with a smile.

"Well, Mrs. Caine, I've left you some cold poached salmon and a salad in the fridge. Mr. Caine won't be home, of course, because he's eating dinner with the governor. If you don't mind, I'm going to leave now. There's a movie showing in town that my husband and I would like to see."

"Please go ahead," Beth said. "You work ridiculously long hours."

"But I'm always paid overtime," the housekeeper pointed out. She took her coat out of a closet and shrugged into it, then reached into a small cupboard by the microwave oven. She extracted a plastic card from inside a recipe book and crossed to the bolted rear door. She pulled on a pair of rubber overshoes, then drew back the bolts on the door and pushed the card into the locking mechanism. There was a faint buzzing sound as the tumblers disengaged. She pushed the door open and tucked the card carefully into her pocket. "You'll refasten the bolts behind me, Mrs. Caine?" she asked.

"Yes, certainly."

Evelyn paused in the doorway to wave goodbye to Kristin. "You and your mommy have a good night," she said. "I'll see you tomorrow morning."

"Bye!" Kristin said. "Bye-bye, 'Lyn."

As soon as the housekeeper was gone, Beth set Kristin on the floor and searched rapidly through the kitchen drawers until she found a plastic bowl and an egg beater for her daughter to play with. Then she glanced out into the hallway. The smell of tobacco smoke and the faint murmur of voices from behind the closed office door reassured her that Bill wasn't likely to return to the kitchen for a few moments at least. Nevertheless, her hand shook as she opened the cupboard next to the microwave and pulled the collection of cookbooks out onto the counter. She thumbed through them rapidly and found spare encoding cards tucked into the covers of two of the books.

Feeling as guilty as if she were stealing some priceless family heirloom, Beth shoved one of the cards into the pocket of her pants. Her throat was dry and her hands were slick with sweat. "Time to go and see Aunt Maria," she said to Kristin, her voice so falsely cheerful that she would have thought even a two-year-old would detect the fraud. "She wants to read you a story before you go to sleep."

Kristin sprang up with alacrity, apparently not noticing the unusual undercurrents in her mother's manner. "Auntie 'Ria is nice." Kristin tucked her hand confidingly into her mother's. "Here in this house is a nice place, Mama."

Beth tried to smile as she stacked the cookbooks back in the cupboard and put the bowl and beater back into the drawer. "Yes," she said. "This is a very nice place to live."

Kristin hopped up the stairs, making a game of each jump. "Me stay here wiv you and wiv Auntie 'Ria." She hesitated in midhop, her expression anxious as she looked at Beth. "Me stay here wiv Man? Wiv you? For ever an' ever?"

"Yes," Beth said, sick with the knowledge of her own deception. "I guess we'll both stay here with your daddy for a while."

"Ouch, Mama! You hurt my hand!"

Beth relaxed her tight grip. "Sorry, honey," she said. "Come on, only one more step. Give a big jump, and then we'll be ready to hear Aunt Maria's story."

Once Kristin was settled for the night, Beth sat on the edge of her bed, a book open on her lap, though she wasn't doing much reading. Kristin liked living at Cobden Farm, Beth acknowledged, facing the fact with considerable reluctance. She liked her newfound Aunt Maria, she enjoyed the company of the housekeeper, and this afternoon she had even flirted mildly with Bill Decker. As for Luke, it was clear that Kristin's earlier hostility toward her father was beginning to change.

In some ways, Beth reflected, Kristin's growing attachment to Cobden Farm merely provided even stronger reasons for leaving Luke as soon as she could. Surely it would be better for everybody if Kristin's roots didn't grow too deep before she was transplanted again. And yet...the truth was that Luke could provide his daughter with so many advantages.

Beth slammed the book closed. The only advantages Luke could provide were financial ones, she reminded herself. Lots of toys, a room with snazzy wallpaper and access to a private beach didn't compensate for a lack of moral values. Did she really want her child to grow up under the guidance of a man whose vote could be bought by anybody with deep enough pockets? A man who had voluntarily associated with violent professional criminals? For all she knew, Luke might still be deeply involved with organized crime in Rhode Island, in which case, it wasn't inconceivable that Kristin might one day find herself—literally—in the line of fire when Luke and his gangster colleagues had a disagreement.

Beth waited until the household was sleeping, then started her packing with renewed determination. Leaving Luke was the right decision, and she wasn't going to question it anymore. Her packing didn't take long. She had performed the same chore so many times during the past two years that it was scarcely more than a few minutes' work to strip her drawers and closet bare. In less than half an hour she had completed Kristin's packing, as well as her own. Dressed in dark pants and a thick sweater, she opened the door of her bedroom, listening intently for any noise or hint of movement.

The house was eerily silent, and the sound of her breathing seemed to reverberate inside her head as she crept down the rear stairs, carrying the two suitcases. She had already decided to go out through a side door that led to the swimming pool. In summer the side entrance carried heavy traffic, but in winter it was scarcely ever used, even during the day.

She slipped the encoding card she had stolen into the lock, stiffening when she heard the faint hum of the tumblers clicking open. Her heart leaped into her throat. Then she realized that nobody was around to hear the tiny betraying noise, and her pulse returned to normal. Quietly, painstakingly, she turned the door handle and stepped outside onto the cement path that skirted the pool and led eventually to the garage that held the car she'd used to drive into Providence.

The grounds immediately surrounding the house were always kept illuminated as a deterrent to burglars. Beth stayed in the shadows as much as possible and, despite the exterior lights, felt confident that nobody saw her. At three o'clock on a November morning her excessive caution was almost unnecessary. She was hardly likely to find Bill Decker or Aunt Maria strolling about the gardens, and Luke was spending the night at the governor's mansion.

She hid the cases behind a workbench at the back of the garage, then rearranged two empty plastic trash barrels and a lawn mower so that the suitcases were almost impossible to detect without prior knowledge that they were there. Dusting off her hands, she slipped out of the garage, automatically glancing around before she ventured back into the brightly lit area around the house.

She froze against the wall when she saw a tall, athletic-looking man emerge silently from the black shadows cast by a cluster of evergreens. When she realized that the man was Luke, relief surged through her. Then the reality of her situation struck her, and she wondered if she might not have preferred to encounter a burglar. If Luke looked in this direction, she would be directly in his line of sight. And if he saw her, all hope of escape would be gone.

She considered retreating into the comparative safety of the garage but rejected the idea almost as soon as it formed. Movement—any movement—would only attract Luke's attention. An owl hooted and Beth instinctively jerked her shoulders. Fortunately she made no sound, but Luke stopped in his tracks, and she huddled against the cold stone wall of the garage, holding her breath, not daring to move. After an endless wait, he reached into the pocket of his windbreaker and pulled something out. He bent his head, and she saw the brief flare of light. Luke was smoking a cigarette, she realized, which she had never seen him do before. Obviously he hadn't noticed her, or he would have done something a great deal more dramatic than lighting a cigarette.

When Luke finally walked off toward the front of the house, her breath returned in a shuddering gasp, and the smell of burning tobacco lingered hauntingly in her nostrils. She waited for half an hour after he'd gone, until her teeth were chattering and her fingers were almost frozen to the wall. Then she crept back to the house. She was panting by the time she had traversed the downstairs hallway and reached the stairs, not from exertion, but from fright. *Face facts,* she instructed herself wryly. *You are definitely not cut out for a life of daring escapes and thrilling intrigue.*

She had to pass Luke's room in order to get to her bedroom. Beth glanced along the upstairs corridor, straining to hear any sound of movement, but no light shone under his door, and the silence was almost deafening in its intensity. The silence should have been reassuring, but the distance between the top of the stairs and her bedroom suddenly seemed enormous. A thousand treacherous miles, where every creaking floorboard was a potential enemy.

She walked on tiptoe, and each breath she drew seemed louder than the one before. She was shaking with nervousness when she finally arrived at her bedroom door. She reached for the doorknob.

"Taking a stroll around the house?" Luke asked casually from the corridor behind her. "Isn't that rather an odd activity at three o'clock in the morning?"

She swung around, then pressed herself back against the door, her heart pounding so hard she couldn't move, even though she knew her cringing posture must have made her appear the picture of guilt. Luke, oddly enough, was smiling, but she could sense the waves of some violent emotion lurking close to the surface of his calm. He was wearing jeans, with a cotton shirt hanging unbuttoned over his belt. A swath of bare, darkly tanned skin stretched from his throat to his waist, and his hair appeared slightly tousled, as if he had just climbed out of bed.

"Cat got your tongue?" Luke inquired politely.

Beth tore her gaze away from his rippling muscles and after what seemed an interminable stretch of silence managed to find her voice. "I couldn't sleep," she mumbled. "I...I went downstairs to make myself a hot drink." It was a pretty feeble excuse, but it was the best she could come up with on the spur of the moment.

Luke gave no sign that he disbelieved her story. "A hot drink?" he asked solicitously. "Are you suffering from the cold? Perhaps we should turn up the heat, although Aunt Maria hasn't complained and she's usually the first person to feel a chill." He covered the few feet of space that remained between them, halting only a couple of inches in front of her.

She gulped, flattening herself against the door in a vain effort to put more space between herself and Luke's threateningly bare chest. "No, no, I'm not cold. Not at all. Don't adjust the thermostat on my account." She was babbling, but as it happened, she spoke nothing but the truth. Her cheeks flamed with heat and her body was on fire, burning with an intoxicating mixture of fear, recklessness and something she chose not to identify.

"But if you're not cold, why on earth are you wearing such a thick sweater? And woolen pants, too. I can't believe you put on all those clothes just to go down to the kitchen." Luke was still smiling, but his eyes had darkened with an all-too-evident trace of mockery. "It seems an incredible story, you know. In fact, if I didn't know that you have no way of letting yourself out of the house, I'd swear that you'd been walking outside in the backyard. But of course, there's no way you could open the doors is there, Beth?"

"N-no. No way." The encoding card tucked deep inside her pocket grew in Beth's imagination until it seemed impossible that Luke should fail to detect its presence. She was almost relieved when he bent over and lifted her hair, pressing his cheek softly against her face. The stubble of his beard rasped faintly against her skin. "You smell of the outdoors," he said huskily. "Night air, cool winds and velvet darkness. Where have you been, Beth?"

"D-downstairs. In the kitchen. I told you."

"Mmm... I know what you told me." His hand grazed slowly along the length of her spine, and she closed her eyes, fighting to keep control of a situation that seemed to be degenerating more rapidly by the moment. She had to stop Luke from asking questions! As long as he didn't have proof of where she had been and what she had been doing, her suitcases might be left undiscovered in the garage. And if her suitcases were safe, she had a decent chance of escaping with Kristin. But without her luggage she would be a prisoner at Cobden Farm, literally unable to afford to leave.

Before he could probe her story any further, she forced herself to look up and meet his eyes. She stroked her forefinger across his mouth, making the movement deliberately seductive. "I may smell of fresh air," she murmured. "But you smell of cigarettes. Or am I imagining it? You never used to smoke."

"You're right. I never smoked until a couple of years ago, when you left me," Luke replied. He flicked his tongue against her finger, and a little too late Beth realized that she might have precipitated something more than she'd bargained for. When she made to move away he reached up and, grasping her hand, turned it over so that he could drop a kiss deep into the hollow of her palm. "I've discovered that frustration causes people to develop all sorts of habits they don't have when they're . . . gratified."

Beth stared at her hand nestled between Luke's lean strong fingers. She forced herself to speak, trying to make her voice light and teasing. "Smoking's hazardous to your health, Congressman. You should give it up before you get really hooked."

His thumb moved caressingly across her palm. "You're quite right, Counselor. But now that you're back at Cobden Farm maybe my frustration level will be lower." His eyes gleamed ebony with laughter in the dimly lit hallway and he leaned forward until his mouth hovered only a breath away from hers. "Who knows, Counselor? Perhaps now that you're home again I'll be able to give up smoking without difficulty."

Beth swallowed hard. "Maybe." She leaned back against the bedroom door, feeling her chest rise and fall in time with the rapid pace of her breathing. Luke stroked his hands along the underside of her breasts, then fanned his fingers over her ribs, stroking gently. She gave up rationalizing what was happening between them and allowed the insidious pleasure of his touch to seep into every pore of her body.

Luke's fingers suddenly stopped weaving their magic. "Beth, what is it? You've turned deathly pale. Are you all right?"

No, she thought, closing her eyes. *No, I'm not all right. I'm in the worst trouble I've been in for more than two years.* She opened her eyes and forced herself to meet his gaze. "I'm fine," she said. "Wonderful. Terrific."

"But I'm not," he murmured harshly. "Let me hold you, Beth. Let me be with you, at least for tonight." His words sank to a whisper as he grasped her shoulders, then slid his hands up to cup her chin. For a single blazing moment they stared into each other's eyes. Then he sighed her name and bent his head, seeking blindly for her mouth.

He kissed her tenderly, covering her lips but not forcing them apart, as if he were offering her one last chance to draw back and renounce the sweetness they both knew was in store. But it was already too late for resistance, too late for common sense. Her body had been crying out for his lovemaking ever since he had taken her to his bed three nights before, and now she craved the consummation of what they had started then.

Her hands came up, clasping together behind his head, and he drew her close, deepening his kiss until their mouths opened in an explosion of mutual need. He shuddered in her arms, and Beth experienced a moment of supreme elation, knowing instinctively that few women—perhaps no other woman—could arouse Luke as immediately and powerfully as she could. She slipped her hands inside his shirt, running her nails over the taut muscles of his back, and his kiss became almost savage in its hunger. His tongue invaded her mouth with hard repeated thrusts and his fingers tightened convulsively in her hair.

He wrenched his mouth away just long enough to pull off her sweater and T-shirt and toss them onto the floor. His eyes darkened when he saw she wasn't wearing a bra. "Dear God," he said. "Each time I see you, Beth, your body looks more beautiful than the time before."

"Hold me," she whispered. "Kiss me, Luke." She lifted her arms and locked her hands behind her head, offering him free access to her body. Her skin was so hot that it burned at his touch, and she cried out helplessly when his mouth closed over one of her nipples. The doorknob pressed into the hollow of her back, but she was scarcely aware of it as he kissed his way back up to her throat and reclaimed her mouth. He thrust his knee between her legs, finally allowing her to feel the full force of his desire, and she arched against him in an instinctive gesture of invitation. She murmured his name like a litany, then whimpered in distress when he suddenly moved away from her.

"We can't stay here," he said jerkily. "Not in the hallway. Let's go into your bedroom."

"Yes." It was all she could manage to say. She was only vaguely conscious of Luke putting his hand behind her knees and sweeping her into his arms. He carried her into the bedroom, and when he lowered her onto the narrow bed she was wild with need for him. He tossed his shirt onto a chair and stepped quickly out of his jeans. When she felt his naked body lying beside her, she gave a long unashamed sigh of pleasure.

Somewhere, buried deep beneath the layers of her delight, she knew that the next day she would regret what she was doing. But when his hands plundered her body and when his tongue thrust deep and hard into her mouth, she forgot everything except the desire he had aroused in her.

At the end, when their bodies were slick with passion, she clung to him, frightened as she felt control begin to slip away from her. It had been so long, and she had never experienced quite this desperate intensity of need.

Luke held her tightly. "Darling, let go," he commanded urgently. "Now, my darling. Don't hold back, I'll keep you safe."

She felt the hot wild surge of his climax, and the waves of ecstasy crashed over her, pulling her down into the darkness where there was only endless agonizing pleasure. And Luke.

CHAPTER NINE

BETH HEARD THE CLICK of the door closing and opened her eyes to find she was alone. The red glow of the digital clock showed that it was already six-thirty in the morning, less than half an hour before Kristin would come bounding into the bedroom, demanding her mother's company for breakfast. It was a good thing that Luke had left, Beth reflected drowsily, or they would have woken up to find Kristin bouncing on their stomachs, no doubt asking some very awkward questions between each bounce.

She sat bolt upright in the bed, dragging the covers with her. Dear heaven, what was the matter with her wits this morning? Answering Kristin's questions was likely to prove the least difficult of the problems facing her. Memories of the previous night's lovemaking returned in a heated rush. What had she done? she asked herself in an agonized whisper. How could she have been crazy enough to think she could seduce her husband and emerge unscathed? True, she had managed to put a stop to his probing questions, but the price of her success was likely to prove intolerably high. Now that she had been reminded of what it was like to experience the joy of making love with Luke, could she ever again accept the bleakness of life without him?

A miniature cyclone hurled itself at the bed, putting a stop to the grim trend of Beth's thoughts. "Me is here, Mama," Kristin announced cheerfully. "Me is dressed." She wriggled one arm, displaying an inside-out sweater pulled on over her pajamas. "Me is a good girl?" she asked hopefully.

"You're a very good girl," Beth replied, kissing her daughter's pink cheek. She drew Kristin into her arms and hugged her tight. "Play with your blocks for five minutes, honey, while I get washed. Then we'll go downstairs and make you some breakfast."

Beth shampooed her hair, then gradually turned the water in the shower to cold. To her relief, the powerful icy spray seemed to restore some of her missing willpower. Last night was an aberration, she told herself over and over. She would not allow Luke's skills as a lover to overcome her basic good judgment. Last night had changed nothing. For Kristin's sake, she had to get away from Cobden Farm.

Her good resolutions were put to the test when she and Kristin came downstairs and found Luke settled at the kitchen table. He was eating cornflakes and chatting cheerily to Evelyn, only the shadows under his eyes hinting at his sleepless night.

"Hello, Man." Kristin wriggled in her mother's arms, staring up at the television, then back at Luke. "You is all gone. Now you come home," she said.

Luke grinned. "I'm not sure what you mean, but I think I'm flattered. I missed you yesterday, honeybun. Did you have a good time? Aunt Maria tells me you and your mommy found a crab on the beach."

Kristin climbed onto the chair beside Luke's. Her chin scarcely reached the top of the table. "Me is bigger than you is, Man," she said. Her idea of conversation didn't always include the notion of answering other people's questions, and yesterday's crab apparently didn't interest her this morning.

Luke looked at her in silence for a moment or so, as if considering how to respond. "No," he said finally, opting for the truth. "You're not as big as I am, Kristin, but I've stopped growing already, and you've hardly begun to grow." He looked up, and his eyes locked briefly with Beth's. "One day I expect you'll be as tall as your mommy, and she's tall for a woman."

"Mama is big. Mama is bigger than you is, Man."

Beth decided this discussion had gone far enough. "Time to eat," she said, lifting Kristin into her special high chair and handing her a bowl of cereal. Beth smiled calmly, proud of the way she managed to conceal the conflicting emotions tearing at her insides. "You'll never grow as big as anybody if you don't eat your breakfast," she added.

Kristin tucked into her cornflakes, using her fingers at least as much as her spoon. Luke watched her for a while, his gaze tender. Then he turned to Beth. "Aren't you planning to have any food this morning?" he asked.

Beth's churning stomach lurched violently a few times, demonstrating exactly what it would do if she tried to eat. "Thanks, but I'm not much of a breakfast eater. I'll just have coffee."

"I was hoping you and Kristin would join me today," Luke said casually. "I have to give a speech this afternoon at the Coast Guard Academy in New London and I thought you might like to come with me. Kristin would probably enjoy the marching bands and the balloons even if she found the speeches a bit of a bore."

Beth took her time pouring a cup of coffee. "New London's in Connecticut, isn't it?" she asked. "When are you planning to leave?"

"Oh, in a little over an hour, I guess. I'm supposed to eat lunch with the dean of students at the Academy, and I have a couple of people to see at Groton Naval Base while I'm in the area. What do you think? Would it be too long a day for Kristin? With the drive and everything, we might not get home much before five or six tonight."

Beth fought against the irrational longing to accept Luke's invitation. But she knew that if she really was serious about getting away from Cobden Farm, she had to make the break as soon as possible, and Luke's absence today offered her a near-perfect opportunity.

"Thanks for thinking of us," she said with forced brightness. "Some other time it might be fun to come with you, Luke, but your schedule today is a bit hectic for Kristin. Her attention span is awfully short."

"Still, I'd like your company. Are you sure I can't persuade you to change your mind?" Luke looked at her searchingly. "Do you have special plans for today, Beth?"

She set her cup down on its saucer, taking care not to let it rattle. "As a matter of fact, I do have plans," she said, thinking rapidly. "Kristin and I both need some new clothes before we accompany you on any official outings. Aunt Maria volunteered to baby-sit for Kristin, so I thought I'd drive into Boston and get myself a couple of decent skirts and blouses. Maybe even a dress or two."

There was an infinitesimal pause. Then Luke smiled heartily. "Well, by all means, you'd better go shopping, Beth." He reached into his hip pocket and pulled out his wallet. He spread an army of credit cards over the kitchen table, tactfully making no reference to the fact that she had sworn only a couple of days earlier that she would never use his money or his credit to buy anything. "Take your pick, my dear. Please choose several outfits so that you'll have no excuse for staying at home next time I make a speech."

Gritting her teeth, hoping he would ascribe her flaming cheeks to embarrassment at having to ask him for money and not to guilt because she was deceiving him, Beth walked over to the table and picked up three or four cards. "Thank you," she said, knowing her voice sounded stiff but unable to do a thing to alter it. "I'll not use these more than I have to."

"Oh, I know that," Luke said softly. "Don't worry, I know exactly how you feel about spending my money. I'll have Bill call so that the stores know you have the right to sign on my cards."

Something in his voice made Beth inexplicably nervous, but unless he was psychic he couldn't possibly know that she was planning to abscond with Kristin, so she forced herself to overcome her fears. "Could you let me have a set of car keys?" she asked. "I may as well make an early start if I'm going to put in a day's shopping."

"Most of the stores don't open until ten," Luke reminded her gently. "And you'll have to get the car keys from Bill. He always keeps track of who's taken which car."

Kristin finished eating her cornflakes. "Me is big now," she interjected. "Look, Man! I growed."

Luke solemnly inspected his daughter. "I can hardly believe it " he said. "But I really do think you look bigger."

Beth couldn't help laughing. "That's because of all the cereal she has sticking to her face," she commented dryly. She took a wad of paper towels and sopped up the remains of Kristin's breakfast, which seemed to be spread almost equally on the chair, on her clothes and in her hair. "Well, I guess I'd better take this young lady upstairs and get her cleaned up." To her relief, her voice sounded only a little strained. "This is obviously going to be one of Kristin's more difficult days. Only seven-thirty in the morning and she's already on to her second set of clothes!"

"Do you have anything for her to change into?"

"Yes, of course. What do you mean?"

Luke pushed back his chair and left the table, ruffling Kristin's sticky hair as he passed by. "Nothing special, Beth. What could I mean?" He paused in the kitchen doorway. "You know, you seem awfully edgy this morning. Is something bothering you?"

"No, nothing special," she said tightly, throwing his own words back at him. "What could be bothering me?"

"I've no idea," he said, smiling. "Well, have a good day shopping, Beth, and I'll see you this evening." He blew a kiss to Kristin, smiled at the housekeeper and strolled quietly out of the kitchen.

Beth waited an hour before she sought out Bill and asked for a set of car keys. She could hear Luke's voice coming clearly from his inner office, but she hadn't expected him to be gone quite this early, and she didn't allow herself to worry. She knew exactly where she could wait until Luke drove off to his appointment at the Coast Guard Academy.

"Are you planning to go out right away, Mrs. Caine?" Bill asked as he handed her the keys to the Oldsmobile she had driven previously.

"Yes, if the car is available."

"No problem. It's parked in its usual spot in the garage."

"Then perhaps you'd be good enough to open the front door for me."

Bill cleared his throat. "Er . . . I'm sorry about this, Mrs. Caine, but I have to ask. Where is Kristin?"

"My daughter is with her great-aunt," Beth said tightly. "Don't worry, it's quite safe for you to let me out of the house."

Bill took a brown plastic card out of his pocket and hurried down the hall. "I apologize for checking up on you," he said as he opened the door. "But you have to see things from Luke's point of view. He's lost the first two years of his daughter's life, and he doesn't want to miss out on anything more."

"I understand Luke's point of view all too clearly," Beth said. "Unfortunately, I'm not sure he understands mine." She thrust the car keys into her jacket pocket. "I imagine I'll be back around four. I've let Evelyn know that I won't be home for lunch.''

"Have a good day, Mrs. Caine." An uncharacteristic note of hesitation crept into Bill's voice. "And please, think again about Luke's feelings for his daughter. He really cares about her, you know."

Beth drove a half mile from the house, then turned the car onto a narrow unpaved road that was cracked and rutted from years of disuse. She parked out of sight of the main road, then got out of the car and crept back to the cover of some overgrown yew trees.

She waited less than fifteen minutes before the familiar dark gray Cadillac passed by. Luke, accompanied by Bill and a man she didn't recognize, was driving in the direction of the interstate highway on his way to Connecticut. She watched the Cadillac until it disappeared from sight, then hurried back to her car. She returned immediately to Cobden Farm, driving through the rear entrance gates and parking inside the garage. She pushed aside the lawn mower and the trash barrels, retrieved her suitcases and stashed them inside the trunk of the Oldsmobile. She glanced at her watch. Still barely nine-thirty. With Luke and Bill Decker en route for Connecticut, she might have a head start of several hours before anybody came looking for her.

She let herself back into the house, then stood absolutely still, adjusting her ears to the subtle sounds of the house. The daily cleaning woman was vacuuming in the living room, and after a while Beth could hear Evelyn moving around in the kitchen. Aunt Maria and Kristin were presumably upstairs. Thank heaven none of the domestic staff happened to be in the hallway. The fewer people who knew she was in the house, the better her chances of getting outside again with her child.

Beth took the stairs two at a time and arrived flushed and out of breath in the nursery, where Maria was reading a magazine at the same time as she kept an eye on Kristin.

"Hi, Mama!" Kristin exclaimed, running across the room and hugging Beth's knees.

"Why hello there," Maria said, looking startled. "That must be the quickest shopping trip on record."

"Oh, my trip's not even started," Beth said quickly. "Can you believe how silly I was? I was onto the highway before I realized that I'd forgotten to put any credit cards into my wallet." She held up her purse. "Anyway, now that I'm properly organized, I'm going to try again."

"I didn't hear the doorbell when you came back," Maria commented.

"Evelyn saw me coming and let me in." Beth turned away to hide her burning cheeks. Despite all the lying she'd had to do, it still didn't come easy.

"Me is thirsty. Can I have a drink?"

"Yes, of course you can." Beth smothered a heartfelt sigh of relief that she didn't need to manufacture an excuse to remove Kristin from Maria's supervision, but it still required every ounce of her acting ability to behave naturally as she held out her hand to her daughter. "Would you like to come downstairs with me to the kitchen? We can both have a drink of apple juice before I go out again."

"I can give her a drink, if you're in a hurry," Maria said.

Beth forced a smile. "You're going to have her all day. I may as well take ten minutes to see that she drinks her juice without spilling it all over the floor. Coming, Kristin?"

"You'll need somebody to let you out of the house again," Maria said.

"No problem. I'll ask Evelyn." Beth swept Kristin up into her arms and, spotting her daughter's security blanket over a chair, managed to scoop that up without making her action too obvious. The teddy bear unfortunately was all the way over on the opposite side of the room. Some things she just hadn't been able to plan for.

Beth walked quickly down the stairs, carrying Kristin and resisting the almost overwhelming impulse to take to her heels and run. When she got downstairs she paused just long enough to listen carefully. Aunt Maria was still in the nursery, the housekeeper was still in the kitchen, and the cleaning woman was now in the dining room. Nobody was in the hallway to see what she was doing. With any luck, she might have half an hour before Aunt Maria came in search of Kristin, and since Luke wasn't scheduled to be at the Coast Guard Academy until noon, it might be a couple of hours before he was informed of what had happened. Beth angled toward the side door, her throat closing so tightly with nerves that she would have gagged if she'd been required to speak.

She slipped the encoding card into the side door and the lock clicked open. "Where is we going?" Kristin asked loudly. "Where is my juice?"

"Shh." Beth clapped her hand over Kristin's mouth and opened the door. The path to the garage looked blissfully deserted. Thank heaven there were no gardeners working on the grounds at this time of year! She hurried to the car and strapped Kristin into the back seat, her fingers shaking so much that she could hardly click the fastener on the seat belt.

"Where is we going, Mama?" Kristin demanded, more loudly this time. Panic thinned her voice as Beth turned the key in the ignition and backed out of the garage without replying. "Where is my teddy? Where is Man? I want my teddy, Mama." She burst into tears. "I want my juice! I want Man!"

Beth's stomach knotted with anguish, but she forced herself to ignore Kristin's sobs as she drove swiftly in the direction of the interstate highway. She planned to cross the

state border into Massachusetts, then double back before
heading southwest. She decided to make Oklahoma or New
Mexico her destination and thought she eventually would
look for permanent work there. She still had her emergency
cash fund of four hundred and sixty-nine dollars, and she
was expert at finding motel owners who were prepared to
give her a few nights' room and board in exchange for unpaid waitress service in the motel dining room. If she could
avoid Luke for a week, even for five days, she was confident that her trail would be hard to pick up. A small blue
Oldsmobile with mud smeared over the license plates wasn't
likely to linger in anybody's memory.

She stopped only once, at a busy gas station about ten
miles from Cobden Farm and only a few miles from the
Massachusetts border. She didn't risk speaking to any of the
attendants. She put a coin into a machine and bought Kristin a container of grape juice. The drink didn't stop Kristin's tears over her missing teddy bear, but after some
persuasion, she agreed to curl up with her security blanket,
and soon sheer exhaustion sent her into a light doze.

Beth was less than three miles from the Massachusetts
border when she first spotted the police car in her rearview
mirror. She estimated that it was a mile away from her, but
it was traveling in the fast lane and gaining on her by the
second. Its overhead lights flashed threateningly, and the
muted blare of its siren drowned out all the other highway
sounds. She glanced down at the dashboard and checked her
speed. She was doing two miles an hour more than the legal
limit, surely not enough to attract the attention of a traffic
cop.

Don't panic, she told herself. *Police cars patrol this
stretch of road all the time*. She fought against the impulse
to floor the accelerator. The last thing she wanted was to
give the driver of the police car a good excuse to pursue her.

Maybe the cop had already cornered his quarry, Beth thought hopefully. She looked into her mirror again and saw that the patrol car was continuing its inexorable pursuit. The red warning light flashed brighter and the sound of the siren became louder as the cars behind her slowed down and pulled over to the right, giving the police car room to pass. It was now less than four hundred yards behind her, and she could see that the driver was not alone.

Slowly, her heart thudding so violently that her body literally shook in rhythm with each beat, Beth lifted her foot from the accelerator and steered the Oldsmobile onto the gravel shoulder. The patrol car cut swiftly in front of her, forcing her to stop. The policeman got out of the car and walked purposefully toward her.

But Beth scarcely noticed the policeman; her gaze was riveted on the other man getting out of the patrol car. Luke. He was still fifteen yards away from her, but even at that distance she could see that his mouth was drawn into a straight harsh line and that his eyes were black with anger. The gravel crunched noisily beneath his feet as he strode toward the car. She mustered every remaining ounce of her courage and stared at him defiantly, but he pulled open the rear door of the Oldsmobile, totally ignoring her presence. The absolute coldness of his expression warmed as he looked down at his daughter, who was rubbing her eyes sleepily and clutching her security blanket. His movements were gentle as he bent down, unfastened the seat belt and swung Kristin up and into his arms.

The child came fully awake as the cold air struck her. "Daddy!" she exclaimed, her mouth curving into a radiant smile. "Daddy, you is here!"

For a long moment Luke stood absolutely still. Then his arms clenched tightly around her chubby stomach and he rested his forehead against hers. "Hi, honeybun," he said softly. "How are you doing?"

"Where is Teddy? Can we go home and see my teddy?"

"We sure can," Luke said. "That's why I'm here. I've come to take you home."

Kristin wriggled excitedly, twisting around to look at her mother. "Daddy's here. Time to go home, Mama."

Beth licked her lips. "Yes," she said. "I see that Daddy is here."

The policeman spoke for the first time. "I'm Sergeant Denney, Mrs. Caine. Would you please get out of the car?"

Beth did as she was asked. Once outside, she leaned against the side of the car because she knew her legs would not have supported her unaided.

"Mrs. Caine, I understand you are a lawyer, so you must know that kidnapping is a federal offense. Your husband has shown me the court order in his possession, forbidding you to remove his daughter from the state of Rhode Island. This road you were driving along leads straight into Massachusetts—and nowhere else. If you had crossed the state line, you would have acted in flagrant defiance of your husband's court order and opened yourself to possible criminal charges."

"He obtained that order under false pretenses," Beth rasped. "It would never stand up in court."

Sergeant Denney sighed. "Mrs. Caine, I don't know all the legal ins and outs of this situation. I do know that your situation could have been a lot worse than it is. Your husband asked for police assistance so that he could overtake you before you crossed the state line. He didn't have to be so generous. He could have asked me to radio one of my colleagues in Massachusetts and warn them you were coming. If he'd done that, the Massachusetts police would have arrested you as soon as you entered their jurisdiction."

Beth flinched and the sergeant's stern expression mellowed slightly. "You and the congressman have a beautiful young daughter, Mrs. Caine. For her sake I recommend you find some better way to resolve your custody dispute than chasing each other around the state highways."

"I appreciate your help, Sergeant Denney," Luke said, shaking the policeman's hand. "And I agree with your advice. I hope my wife and I can reach an agreement about Kristin some time in the very near future."

The sergeant touched his hat. "Glad to have been of assistance, Congressman. That was an excellent bit of work you did getting those students out of El Gabon. My wife and I have a son who's a freshman in Kingston this fall, and we know how we'd feel if he got caught in the cross fire of two bunches of crazies."

"I think the media exaggerated my role in the rescue," Luke said.

"I doubt it," Sergeant Denney said. "Everyone in the police department knows how much you've done for this state, Congressman, and how you wouldn't allow any publicity. We all hope you'll decide to run for senator next year."

Luke smiled with real warmth. "Thank you, Sergeant. I'm definitely thinking about it."

"Me is cold," Kristin said, tugging Luke's hand. "Me and Mama want to go home."

"And I have to get back to work," Sergeant Denney said. "Good afternoon, Congressman, ma'am." He turned and walked quickly to the patrol car.

Luke returned Kristin to her seat in the back of the car. Then he straightened and spoke directly to Beth for the first time since he'd caught up with her.

"Get in," he said, jerking his head toward the front passenger seat. "And if you're smart, you won't say *anything*."

CHAPTER TEN

BILL DECKER, Aunt Maria and the housekeeper were waiting anxiously in the hallway when Luke carried Kristin into the house, with Beth trailing in the rear. They greeted Kristin with hugs, kisses and cries of delight. In contrast, they couldn't have greeted Beth with less enthusiasm if she had been a reincarnation of Lizzie Borden carrying her ax.

Maria's gaze skimmed disdainfully over Beth, successfully demoting her to the status of a nonperson. "Thank God you caught up with them!" she said to Luke, still hugging Kristin and smothering her with kisses. "Dear God, I'd never have forgiven myself if you'd lost your child again."

"I've already told you not to blame yourself," Luke said quietly. "I knew what Beth was planning to do, Maria, and I accept full responsibility for allowing it to happen."

Beth's head jerked up in shock. "You knew?" she whispered.

"Of course I knew." Luke's mouth thinned contemptuously. "I watched you hide your getaway luggage in the garage. Even if I hadn't seen you doing that, you gave yourself away this morning when you said you were going shopping and asked me for the loan of some charge cards. That was a bad mistake, Beth. We both know that you'd wear thrift shop rejects before you'd use my money to buy yourself new clothes."

"If you knew what I was planning to do, why didn't you stop me?"

He eyed her cynically. "Let's just say that it suited my purposes to let you make a run for it."

"You deliberately set me up," she breathed. "You never intended to visit the Coast Guard Academy, did you?"

"No, at least not today. Although I do happen to have a speech scheduled there in the week after Thanksgiving."

Kristin decided that she was bored with the conversation, which she didn't understand. "Me get down now, Daddy," she said, wriggling out of his arms. "Want to play."

"So you've learned to say daddy!" the housekeeper exclaimed, smiling delightedly. "Well, now, that's a step in the right direction, young lady."

"I'll agree to that," Bill said jovially.

Kristin, relishing her position at the center of so much fond attention, reached up and clutched Bill's hand. "Hi, Decker!" she said. "Me is home."

"And it's great to have you here," he replied, patting her hand. His pale face looked more animated than Beth had ever seen it before. "How are you doing, little lady? My, are we glad to see you back home again!"

"Me is big, not little."

"So you are, and getting bigger all the time."

"Guess what, Kristin! I have some ice cream waiting for you in the kitchen," the housekeeper said. "Is it all right, Mr. Caine, if I take your daughter and give her some lunch? It's getting really late and she only had a bowl of cereal for breakfast."

"Ice cream is nice," Kristin pronounced before her father could deny her the treat. "Mama, do you want some ice cream wiv me?"

Three pairs of eyes turned and glared antagonistically at Beth. Only Luke avoided looking at her as he bent down and spoke to Kristin.

"Your mother and I don't have time to eat the ice cream," he said. "We have to go out, sweetheart. We're going for a drive in the car and we won't be home tonight. But we'll be back soon, I promise, and in the meantime, your Aunt Maria is going to take care of you."

Kristin's mouth crumpled as she twisted away from Luke and ran to clutch her mother's knees. "Mama, I don't want you to go away! Stay here wiv me!"

"Sweetheart, don't worry, I'm not—"

"Your mommy will be back very soon," Luke interrupted, gently disengaging Kristin's feverish hold on her mother's knees and restoring her to the housekeeper. "We're not going very far, honeybun, and we'll telephone you tonight." He tickled her softly under her chin, making her giggle, albeit a touch reluctantly. "You know what we're going to do? We're going to pick out a new friend for your teddy bear. We're going to find a girl teddy bear, with a pretty yellow dress to match your teddy's smart yellow jacket."

Kristin's attention was successfully diverted. "Where is my teddy?" she asked. "Auntie 'Ria, do you have my teddy?"

"I'll go and get him right now," Maria said. "He's waiting in your room. He sure will be glad to know you're back."

"We'll get Teddy a dish of ice cream, shall we?" suggested the housekeeper. "Does he like vanilla?"

The subtleties of flavor were entirely lost on Kristin, who considered one variety of ice cream quite as good as another. "Teddy likes ice cream," she said. She thought for a moment, then added, "Blue ice cream."

Luke leaned forward and gave his daughter a quick kiss. "I'm sure Evelyn has lots of blue ice cream," he said. "Go with her and see."

Beth swallowed the scream of protest that was forming in her throat and forced herself to smile as she followed Luke's example and kissed her daughter goodbye.

"I'll see you soon, Kristin," she said, vowing silently that she'd keep her promise, whatever contrary plans Luke might have in store for her. She knew, however, that for her daughter's sake she ought not to create a scene, so she turned to the housekeeper, trying to sound calm and matter of fact as she gave a few last-minute instructions. "Kristin is allergic to strawberries," she said, "and too much chocolate upsets her stomach."

The housekeeper nodded. In contrast to her friendliness of the day before, her manner was now glacial. "Very good, Mrs. Caine. Most young children are allergic to strawberries, so naturally I wouldn't have given Kristin any. You can trust me to see that *Mr. Caine's daughter* isn't given food that disagrees with her." She allowed time for her emphasis to sink in, then added, "Mr. Caine knows that I'm quite experienced with planning menus for young children."

The housekeeper held out her hand to Kristin, her expression once again relaxing into friendly warmth. "I can hear your Aunt Maria coming and I'll bet she's bringing your teddy bear downstairs. Are you ready to eat your lunch, honey?"

"Ready," Kristin agreed, skipping happily toward the kitchen, her tears already forgotten. "Bye-bye, Mama. Bye, Daddy."

Bill Decker waited until the child and the housekeeper were out of earshot before speaking. "Luke, the chief of police called. He wants to know if you intend to press charges against . . . He, um, wondered if you're planning to notify the court about today's incident. Apparently it affects the kind of report Sergeant Denney has to file."

"I haven't decided yet whether I'll press charges," Luke said. His eyes glittered briefly with some emotion Beth couldn't quite identify. "I'll be in touch with the police chief as soon as I know."

"Right. I'll give him a call and say you'll get back to him. Also, the news director from Channel 8 has been on the phone nonstop. Someone in Washington tipped him off that the President's asked you to head up a delegation to El Gabon. So far I've managed to stop them sending a minicam unit over to stake out the house."

"Good work," Luke said. "Stall them for me, Bill, if you possibly can. I don't want TV crews anywhere near this place until Kristin is more accustomed to living here."

"I'll do my best. In the meantime, shall I confirm or deny the story?"

"Say that any announcement has to come from the White House."

"Fair enough. Where are you going to be, Luke, in case I really need to get in touch?"

"I'm going to the cottage."

"Fine. I won't contact you unless it's a real emergency." Bill still avoided looking at Beth, and Luke's statement about where he planned to go suggested that both he and Bill had forgotten the fact of her existence. She should have known better. She made a slight movement in the direction of the front door, and Luke's hand jerked out, seizing her wrist and clamping her against his side.

"Anything else, Bill?" Luke made no effort to disguise the fact that he was using his physical strength to prevent Beth from moving.

Bill's gaze slid carefully over Beth and fixed itself on the middle distance. "Er...nothing else important. I'll see that the Cadillac is brought out front. Do you know how long you'll be gone?"

"I'm not sure. Not more than a couple of days, for Kristin's sake." Luke shifted his grip to Beth's elbow and steered her relentlessly toward the front door. "I'll call tonight around seven, before Kristin goes to bed."

Beth waited until they were outside the house before she spoke. "I suppose it's useless for me to say that, wherever you're planning to go, I don't want to come with you."

Luke instantly dropped his hold on her arm. "It's not useless at all," he said. His mouth twisted into a mocking smile. "If you want to leave, please feel free to take your suitcase and be on your way."

She couldn't look at him. "You know I can't go anywhere without Kristin."

"Then for both our sakes, let's be quite clear about my intentions," he said, his voice flat. "Unless you come with me to the cottage, I'm filing kidnapping charges against you. And I have half a dozen witnesses, including a police sergeant, to back up my case."

"That's why you let me get away this morning, isn't it?" she said bitterly. "I've been dumb enough to hand you the perfect blackmail weapon."

"That's part of the reason," he said curtly. "The other side of the coin is that—despite all the evidence to the contrary—I hoped I could trust you. It's crazy, but I still hoped against hope that you weren't going to betray me. I should've known better. Nothing you've done in the past two and a half years has given me any reason to trust you."

She started to laugh, and once she started it seemed impossible to stop. "*You* can't trust *me*!" she gasped. "Oh God, I think that's probably funny."

Luke didn't bother to ask her meaning. Grim-faced, he thrust her into the Cadillac, then walked quickly around to the driver's seat. By the time he turned out of the driveway her laughter had turned to tears, and by the time they reached the highway she was sobbing uncontrollably.

"Here." He handed her a wad of tissues. She took it without comment, blew her nose and finally managed to bring her tears under control. It had been a long time since she had cried so unrestrainedly, Beth realized.

"Do you want to tell me what that outburst was all about?" he asked when she had finished mopping up with the tissues.

"I don't think so," she responded wearily. "Why won't you accept the fact that you and I have nothing to say to each other, Luke?"

His mouth twisted into a hard unyielding line. "Keep something in mind, Beth, before you decide to be too uncooperative. I've waited two and a half years to find out why you hid my child from me, and after this morning's little kidnapping episode, I've decided I'm not prepared to wait any longer. I want some answers, and this time I'm planning to get them. One way or another."

Beth stared out the window, watching the gnarled brown trunks of oak and chestnut trees flash by. Luke headed the car for Sakonnet, and she shivered despite the warmth fanned out by the powerful car heater. The cottage where he was taking her was located on a stretch of coastline that was virtually deserted at this time of year. What was he planning to do with her? And what was she going to do if he demanded answers to his questions before he would allow her to see Kristin again? Was she going to tell him why she had run away that summer night more than two years ago? Could she risk telling him what she had discovered about his connections to the Timberline Construction Company and about the bribes she knew he had taken? Once the truth lay open and exposed between them, it could never be hidden again. What would Luke do once he knew that she was aware of his criminal activities? What could either of them do? she reflected helplessly. They would both be caught in a hideous trap, with Beth honor bound to report what she knew to the authorities and Luke compelled to prevent her.

"We're here," he said about an hour later, parking on a rough patch of gravel outside a white clapboard cottage. "Wait on the porch while I get your bag."

The front door opened straight into a small sparsely furnished living room dominated by a fieldstone fireplace and a long loose-cushioned sofa. The air inside the cottage struck Beth somewhat chill after the heat of the car, but there was no hint of sea dampness.

"It shouldn't take long for the place to warm up," Luke said. He set Beth's suitcase at the foot of an open staircase that led to the second floor. "I come here whenever I get the chance, so I keep the place stocked with food and I leave the thermostat set at sixty."

"I'm not cold," Beth said tersely. "Could you tell me where the bathroom is?"

"Yes, upstairs next to the bedroom. On the ground floor, there's just this living room and a kitchen. Then there's a utility room sort of tacked on the back. Shall I take your bag upstairs for you?"

"Don't bother, thank you, I can manage."

The bathroom was unexpectedly luxurious, with double sinks, a whirlpool attachment in the giant tub, and thick-piled, wall-to-wall carpeting. The bedroom, similarly carpeted, contained only one bed, an oversized thing with a panel of switches built into the headboard. Anybody lying in bed could switch off the lights, adjust the TV and fine-tune the stereo without stirring from the comfort of the king-size mattress. It was all too evident, Beth reflected bleakly, that the bed was an instrument of seduction at least as much as a place to sleep. When Luke shed his responsibilities and got away from it all, he obviously made sure he had an entertaining bedmate to enliven his solitude. She wondered if he imported his playmates from Washington or whether he discovered them locally.

Either way the pictures summoned by her overactive imagination were unbearably painful, and she went quickly back downstairs, anxious to get away from the bedroom. She found Luke kneeling in front of the fireplace, a lock of ebony hair falling over his tanned face, his strong hands easily spanning a thick log, which he picked up and placed on the pile of crumpled newspaper. She watched him in silence, not wanting to acknowledge that the mere sight of him was sufficient to turn her mouth dry and make her heart pound heavily against her ribcage.

He struck a long match and held it to one corner of the newspaper. Flame leaped up and engulfed the kindling, then settled into a constant steady glow. The sharp aromatic tang of burning pine scented the room, and Beth smiled ironically. Trust Luke to get the fire alight with only one match! She couldn't remember a single occasion when he failed at something he set out to do.

He stood up, looking at her with an expression that was hard to define. "I'll wash my hands in the kitchen," he said after a brief pause. "Would you like me to get you a drink while I'm there?"

"Please. What do you have?"

"Coke, a selection of diet sodas, white wine, beer."

"Some white wine would be nice. It's been a very long day."

"Chablis okay?"

"Chablis would be fine."

"I've already put a couple of frozen dinners into the oven, since we both missed lunch. They'll be ready in half an hour."

Luke's mention of food made Beth remember that she hadn't eaten anything all day. She shrugged. "I'm not very hungry," she said truthfully.

"Nevertheless it's probably a good idea to eat some dinner."

He went into the kitchen and she paced restlessly for a few minutes, then crossed the room to look out of the window. It was only four o'clock, but already the light was fading and the deserted beach appeared desolate, almost menacing, in the gathering darkness. The ocean was no more than thirty yards away, a heaving quilt of gray flecked with white. Even through the closed window she could hear the waves breaking with thunderous power against the pebble-strewn shore.

"Beth, here's your wine."

She hadn't realized that he had come back from the kitchen and she turned swiftly. He was much closer than she had expected—so close in fact that she could see the lines of fatigue that etched a faint frown between his eyes and smell the tang of wood smoke that clung to his shirt.

She took the glass from him and, moving quickly to the other side of the room, curled up in a corner of the big overstuffed sofa. He followed her but didn't sit down. Instead he stood sipping his wine and staring broodingly into the heart of the fire. He had discarded his jacket and shirt in favor of a loose-fitting cotton sweater, and the flickering flames silhouetted his muscular body, outlining the broad strength of his shoulders and the firm clear-cut angles of his profile.

The silence in the room began to seem oppressively loud. Luke tossed another log onto the fire, then straightened and turned slowly toward her. A quiver of awareness coursed through her when his gaze moved to her lips. "Beth," he said quietly. "Why do you keep running away from me?"

She intended to reply with as much control as he had shown in asking the question. She drew in a deep calming breath—but suddenly two long years of turmoil, fear and anguish exploded into a violent burst of rage. She sprang to her feet, hurling her wine glass at the fire and feeling a primitive satisfaction when she saw it shatter into a dozen shimmering pieces. The wine hissed as it hit the blazing logs, turning their flames from scarlet to blue.

"Why do I keep running away?" she yelled at Luke, hating him, because even now she had to fight against the impulse to run to his side and beg to be taken in his arms. "I'll tell you why I keep running, Luke Caine! I do it because I can't bear to live with you. I run because I despise you and every rotten crooked deal you've ever made." She dashed her hand across her eyes and lowered her voice to a harsh painful murmur. "And—God help me—I run because I can't seem to stop wanting you when we're together."

She started for the door, but he caught up with her easily, seizing her from behind, his strong hands grasping her waist and preventing her from escaping.

"I want you, too," he said huskily, pulling her back against his thighs. "Feel what you do to me just by being in the same room." He bent his head and kissed the pulse that beat frantically at the base of her throat. "Tell me, Beth, is this what you can't stop wanting? The touch of my mouth against your skin? Or is it the touch of my hands unbuttoning your blouse? Or the touch of my fingers caressing your breasts?" He kissed her lingeringly. "Tell me, Beth, is this what you can't stop wanting?"

Her hands clung to his shoulders, her nails digging into his flesh as she gathered up every fragile drop of her willpower. "No," she whispered. "Don't do this to me, Luke. Last night was a terrible mistake and we mustn't repeat it. Let me go, Luke. This isn't what I want."

"Isn't it?" he queried softly. "Then why haven't you moved from my arms?"

"I don't know! Why does it feel so right when you hold me?"

"Because it is right. For both of us."

He bent to kiss her and she whispered a protest that they both knew lacked any real meaning. Her fingers clenched in his hair as he unfastened the last few buttons of her blouse and slowly pushed it off her shoulders. His hands stroked enticingly over her slender throat, trailing downward to cup her breasts and lift them toward his mouth. The blaze in his eyes darkened to a deep smoldering fire. "Don't fight me, Beth," he murmured, "because you won't win. I'm going to carry you over to the sofa and make love to you until you beg me to possess you."

Desire washed over her in a relentless wave. She closed her eyes, hovering somewhere between despair and ecstasy as his fingers teased her nipples, swiftly transporting her into a world where his powerful hands and hard caressing mouth were the only realities.

"Luke, don't do this to me," she pleaded. "Please...don't...make...me...want...you."

"It's too late. You already want me, Beth, just as I want you. Last night only reminded us of how much we've been missing." She trembled when he deliberately thrust against her stomach, vividly demonstrating the effect she had upon him.

"Does it give you a feeling of power to know how much I need you?" he asked roughly. "To know that I wake up every day with a nagging pain in my gut, aching to hold you? Touch me, Beth, and feel what you've done to me. Does it give you a feeling of power to know that I burn for a woman who hates me so much that she runs away every time I get close to her?"

"I have no power," she whispered, shivering as his fingers traced a line of fire down her body and slipped inside the waistband of her skirt. "Oh God, Luke, when I'm with you, all I have is weakness."

"Then let me hold you," he said, his voice losing some of its harshness. "Come to me, Beth. Let me give you some of my strength."

She swayed toward him and they clung for a moment, until he lifted her up in his powerful arms and carried her upstairs to the bedroom. Placing her gently on the bed, he stripped off her clothes and ran his hands over her breasts and hips in a wordless declaration of possession. Then he shed his own clothes, dropping them in a crumpled heap on the floor, and joined her on the mattress. She waited in an agony of longing as his mouth slowly descended toward her lips.

"Oh Beth, how I want you," he said, kissing her with a tormented urgency that echoed the clamoring needs of her own body. Her head fell back, and she wound her arms around his neck, clinging to him as he entered her. She was too lost in physical sensation to be shocked when she heard the thin animal cry that ripped from her throat as he moved inside her. He captured her hands and held them high above her head so that her body arched instinctively in rhythm with his.

At the last moment he stilled his movements, holding her tantalizingly on the very edge of release. "Do you want me, Beth?" he whispered, cupping her breasts with sure hard fingers. "Do you want me to make you feel the way you did last night?"

It was hopeless to deny the truth when he could read it in every shuddering line of her body. "Yes."

"Then say the words. I need to hear you say them."

"What words?"

"You know what they are."

Her breath came in small panting gasps. "I . . . want you. Please, Luke, make love to me."

His tongue nuzzled her ear, and his voice softened with a hint of tender laughter. "Try again, dear heart. You almost have it right."

"I . . . love you, Luke. Please make love to me—now."

His eyes blazed with unmistakable—and very masculine—triumph, and he drove into her with a raw power that shattered her senses, sweeping her over the precipice into the free-fall of ecstasy.

It was only later, as she drifted off to sleep in his arms, that Beth recognized the frightening truth of what she had said. She loved Luke. She had run so hard and so far during the past two and a half years because she was trying desperately to avoid the truth. But she couldn't avoid the truth any longer. Whatever his faults, she loved her husband. She always had, and she was very much afraid that she always would.

CHAPTER ELEVEN

BETH REACHED OUT HER HAND, but she encountered only rumpled sheets and a vast lonely emptiness. Memories of the previous night swept inexorably into her mind, and she rolled over, burying her face in the pillow. Sunlight was streaming into the room, indicating that the morning was far advanced, but she wished she could fall asleep again; she wasn't ready to acknowledge the reality of what had taken place last night with Luke.

Closing her eyes was not a very effective shield against images that remained disturbingly clear and vivid. How, she asked herself, had she and Luke fallen back so easily into the familiar destructive patterns of their marriage? Throughout their relationship she had always forgotten her problems in the passion of his lovemaking, and the previous two nights had been no exception to the old rule. She had learned nothing in the long months they had been apart. As far as she was concerned, Luke was still irresistible.

She sat up in the huge bed and looked around the bedroom. Something in the quality of the silence surrounding her suggested that Luke was nowhere inside the cottage. How typical it was of their relationship, she thought despairingly, that she should wake up to find him gone. At night he silenced her questions with the devastating power of his kisses. In the cool light of morning he took care never to be availabe for discussion.

She showered, dressed in jeans and a sweater, and went downstairs to the kitchen. Luke had left coffee in the percolator, and it smelled enticing. She poured herself a cup and glanced out of the window as she tried to plan what to do next.

The sun was shining with rare brilliance for this late stage of the year, and she spotted Luke's solitary figure walking down by the ocean, at least half a mile from the cottage. She turned away from the window, and her eye was caught by the glint of metal gleaming in the sunlight. Keys, she thought abstractedly. Luke had left his car keys on the counter.

She picked them up and ran upstairs, almost without conscious realization of what she was doing. She grabbed her purse and threw clothes into her suitcase with maniacal speed, then tore back downstairs and rushed outside. The Cadillac was exactly where Luke had left it the previous afternoon, parked on a patch of gravel only a few yards from the front porch.

The doors weren't even locked. She tossed her suitcase onto the rear seat and shoved the keys into the ignition. Pushing the gear shift hurriedly into drive, she gunned the accelerator, indifferent to the spray of gravel from beneath the back wheels as she roared off down the narrow lane.

She hadn't reached the intersection with the main road before she slowed her reckless pace to a mere crawl and finally brought the car to a halt at a point where the grass shoulder offered a natural parking spot. Shaken, she turned off the ignition, and assessed the stupidity of what she was doing. Her movements over the past fifteen minutes or so had been little short of demented. Where was she running to? How did she expect to claim Kristin? Most important of all, what would she prove by running away again? The reality of last night's lovemaking couldn't be wiped out simply because she refused to face Luke in the morning.

Beth got out of the car and leaned against the hood, forcing herself to assess her situation rationally. Somehow, somewhere along the line, she had lost the habit of facing up to her problems. She tried to solve anything unpleasant by taking to her heels and running away as fast as she could. But the trouble was that some problems wouldn't disappear no matter how far a person ran. Her problem was that she loved a man who was a crook. That truth would remain whether she confronted it here in Rhode Island or spent the rest of her life running away from it.

Even if by some miracle she managed to snatch Kristin away from Cobden Farm, did she really want to spend the rest of her life hiding in one ugly furnished apartment after another? She and Kristin would never be able to lead normal lives, Beth realized, until she faced up to the past and confronted Luke with all that she knew about him.

She drew in a final invigorating breath of sea air and returned to the car and, reversing quickly, drove back in the direction she had come. Five minutes later, she parked the car and let herself into the cottage.

Luke was sitting on the sofa in the living room, a book open on his lap and a Bach cantata playing in the background. A roaring fire blazed in the hearth, and the spartan room looked unexpectedly welcoming.

Luke glanced up at the sound of her entrance, and for a fleeting instant, she saw relief shine naked in his eyes.

"It's good to see you," he said. "When I left those car keys on the kitchen counter, I wasn't sure you'd come back."

"I'm all through with running away," she replied quietly. Beth moved farther into the room, thrusting her hands into the pockets of her jeans. "We have to talk, Luke."

"Yes, we do." He got up from the sofa, walked over to the fire and poked randomly and somewhat inexpertly at the burning logs. With a jolt of astonishment she realized that her husband—the sophisticated politician who was never at a loss for words—was as nervous as she was.

"Luke," she said softly. "I want to explain why I left you that night in July two years ago."

He braced his shoulders, but didn't say anything for a few moments. At last he put down the poker with exaggerated care and turned to face her. "I would very much like to know why you left," he said.

"I ran away for one simple and clear-cut reason," she said. "But there were lots of other problems in our marriage, Luke. We never had time to talk and we were never alone together except when we were in bed. Looking back on our marriage, I can't remember ever finishing a conversation with you. Either your mother would interrupt or the phone would ring or Bill would contact you with an urgent message. That was on the rare nights when your mother wasn't entertaining twenty-five people for cocktails and another ten for dinner. We had no privacy, Luke, no real life together. Even if I hadn't run away, our marriage would have been in big trouble."

"You're probably right, although I think we could have worked it out. After all, we did love each other."

"Yes," she said. "We loved each other once."

"Once?" he repeated. "Is our feeling for each other all in the past, Beth?" He looked at her steadily. "Last night you said you loved me."

She turned away. "People say all sorts of things they don't mean in the heat of passion."

"People may but you don't."

She knotted her hands together so tightly that her fingers turned numb. "A marriage needs more than . . . more than sexual attraction to hold it together, Luke. We respond to each other physically, but it's not enough."

"I think there's more than physical attraction between us," he said quietly. He walked over to her side and, taking her hands, held them in a warm clasp he kept deliberately nonsexual. "I think we could have a good future together if we worked at it, Beth. For our daughter's sake, if for no other reason, do you want to give it a try?"

She remained silent and he smiled coaxingly. "I've reformed over the past two years, you know. You might say I've finally realized the error of my chauvinist, workaholic ways. I no longer believe that the world's going to stop revolving on its axis if I take a day off and spend it loafing with my family."

She couldn't resist smiling back at him. "But you probably will think Washington will slide into the Potomac if you're not there to keep it in place."

He grinned. "Not true," he said. "I'm here today, even though I'm supposed to be leaving for El Gabon. Doesn't that prove I'm a reformed character?"

She winced at his choice of words. "Perhaps."

"Beth, please think about what I'm asking. If you're willing to give our marriage another try, I guarantee we can work out a better basis than we had before. The last time we didn't leave ourselves enough room to communicate. This time we'll make sure that we have plenty of space in our schedules for talking. Besides, we have Kristin to think of now. In your heart of hearts, you know that I only want to do what's best for her."

She tensed, knowing that the moment had come when she could no longer delay telling the truth about why she had run away. "I haven't explained things properly," she said tautly. "Luke, you don't understand. I wasn't so immature that I left Cobden Farm for the sort of reasons we've just been discussing. I didn't break up our marriage because you were a chauvinist or even because your mother deliberately made life difficult for me." She drew in a deep breath, forcing herself to meet his eyes. "I left because I discovered that you and Giuseppe Bellini had taken hundreds of thousands of dollars in bribes from crooked officials."

"You left because of what?"

Her hands were slippery with sweat, and she wiped them nervously on her jeans. "I left because if I'd stayed, I would have had to present evidence to the D.A. that connected you with the Timberline Construction Company scam." She swallowed hard. "I left because I'd already had to pull one detective from the case in order to protect you. I couldn't square it with my conscience if I had to conceal any more evidence and so I ran."

"You ran away to protect me," he murmured, pressing a hand to his forehead. "You left on July sixteenth. Dammit, let me think! What evidence could you possibly have uncovered about Peppe and me? What the hell happened on July sixteenth to make you run?"

She felt sick to her stomach. "Allow me to jog your memory," she said dully. "You went to the Greenhouse Restaurant in Massachusetts to discuss your terms for helping the Timberline people expand their lousy corrupt building operations into the state of Pennsylvania. In case you've forgotten, you suggested that a quarter of a million dollars might be a reasonable sum for your services. Paid into your numbered, tax-free Swiss bank account, of course." Her mouth twisted at the bitter memory. "Selling out the citizens of Rhode Island apparently came a whole lot cheaper. You were only paid a hundred thousand dollars to grease the wheels of corruption in your home state."

Luke's face was a stark unrelieved white. "How the hell did you get all that information?" he asked harshly.

He was denying nothing. She felt tears gather in a thick pool at the back of her throat, but she forced herself to continue the painful story. "It came originally from my investigation of Uncle Peppe. I know the D.A. ordered me off the case, Luke, but the local police department had been conducting an investigation of its own and they'd planted an undercover operative in Uncle Peppe's office. Detective Pirelli called me during the second week of July and said he had solid information that the 'big boss' from Washington was flying in to discuss the terms of a deal with the local Timberline people. Somehow, Luke, I just knew you were going to be that 'big boss.'''

"I see." He gave an odd little laugh. "In fact, you had me pegged as the villain of the piece even before you uncovered your so-called evidence."

She closed her eyes. "I wanted it to be somebody else. Oh God, Luke, do you think I wasn't praying that it wouldn't be you?''

"Why pray?" he asked. "Did you think it would take a miracle to prove me innocent?" His mouth twisted into an angry self-mocking line. "Your opinion of me isn't very flattering."

"All the evidence pointed to you, Luke," she said wearily.

"From your perspective, I guess that's true," he said. "All the evidence pointed to me, and yet you never turned in your files." He crooked his finger under her chin and tilted her face up for his inspection. "Even after your worst fears were confirmed, you didn't tell the D.A. what you'd discovered. I turned up at the Greenhouse Restaurant, and you heard me negotiate a bribe of a quarter of a million dollars but you didn't tell anybody."

Her cheeks grew hot with shame. "No," she said, pulling away from him in an effort to hide the extent of her self-disgust. "No, I didn't tell the D.A. what I'd discovered. I compromised every principle I valued by leaving Cobden Farm without telling anybody what I knew, but I can't do that again. Luke, tell me the truth, please. It's really important. Have you...have you cut your connections to those people since Peppe died?''

"Don't beat around the bush, Beth. Say what you mean. You want to know if I'm still taking bribes from criminals.

You want to know if I'm still lining my pockets at the expense of the citizens I've sworn to represent.''

She nodded, keeping her head averted.

"No," he said tightly. "I'm not taking bribes from anybody, Beth, I swear it." His hands grasped her lightly around the waist, compelling her to turn around, and he brushed away the tears that trembled on the edge of her lashes. "Beth, my sweet love, why didn't you tell me what you'd seen at the Greenhouse Restaurant?"

She hesitated. "I was afraid," she admitted at last.

"Afraid? Of me?" There was no mistaking the pain in his voice. "You really thought I might harm you?"

"No, never that. But I was scared of what Uncle Peppe and his associates might do. He ran with a vicious crowd of criminals, Luke."

He looked down at her, his expression unreadable. "And you didn't trust me to protect you?"

"If the people in Uncle Peppe's crowd had known what I'd discovered, I don't think anybody could have guaranteed my safety."

There was a moment of silence. Then Luke spoke softly. "That's what the D.A. and the FBI were afraid of," he said. "That's why I was absolutely forbidden to tell you what was going on in my investigation. The FBI people insisted that ignorance was your best protection."

"The FBI forbade you to tell me what was going on?" Beth held herself perfectly still, not wanting to trust the wild run of hope that coursed through her body. "What exactly do you mean, Luke?"

"I was never taking bribes, Beth, or helping criminals to build substandard bridges. What you heard in that restaurant was part of an ongoing FBI investigation. About four months before you left me, Uncle Peppe found out he was dying. Almost simultaneously he was approached by the people behind the Timberline Company. They asked him to help set up their illegal operations here in Rhode Island. It wasn't the first time Peppe had been asked to arrange pay-offs for corrupt officials, and I suspect he'd accepted more than once. However, Peppe wasn't quite as black as you've always wanted to paint him. True, he helped launder a lot of dubious funds, and true, he made a specialty of defend-ing wealthy criminals that he and everybody else knew were guilty. But the fact is our constitution guarantees the pro-tection of the law to everybody, not just to the good guys, and Peppe was doing nothing illegal in defending people he knew were guilty.''

"Luke, please don't digress. This is too important. What happened when the Timberline people approached Peppe?''

"He stalled, told them their plans sounded great, then came to me. He chose me because we were related and also because I happened to be Chairman of the House Select Committee on Organized Crime.''

"And what did you do when he told you about Timber-line's plans?''

He looked at her consideringly, his eyes reflecting more than a trace of bitterness. ''Well, I sure as hell didn't agree to take any bribes. In fact Peppe didn't offer me any. The last thing he wanted was to spend the final six months of his life helping a bunch of criminals, and he suggested that we should approach the FBI and cooperate with the federal government in setting up some sort of an investigation.''

Beth sat down on the sofa with a decided bump, trying to digest the information Luke was giving her. A great many events from the summer two years ago began to take on a whole new significance. ''No wonder the D.A. didn't want me to investigate Peppe!'' she exclaimed. ''Are you telling me that the evidence the local police uncovered incriminat-ing you and Peppe was all deliberately planted?''

"Yes,'' he said quietly. ''That's precisely what I'm tell-ing you.''

"And when I heard you accepting those bribes, you were involved in an official government investigation?''

"Yes,'' he repeated. "The whole FBI operation was set up to make me seem like the villain of the piece. Peppe went back to the head of the Timberline Company and told him that I was in deep financial difficulty and ripe for a payoff. He pointed out that I was very ambitious and anxious to build up campaign funds prior to my run for the Senate. The Timberline people had no trouble accepting Peppe's word that I was desperate for money. The FBI opened a numbered bank account in Switzerland, and the Timberline Company started to make regular payments into 'my' account. In the meantime Peppe and I walked around wired for sound. The tapes that Peppe recorded formed the backbone of the prosecution's case when the Timberline people were brought in for trial.''

"Oh Luke,'' Beth breathed. "You were putting your life on the line every time you went near those people.''

"Not really. I met them only in public places, and they had no reason to suspect me. Fortunately, criminals always find it easy to believe that other people are as evil as they are, and they never doubted that I was every bit as corrupt as I claimed to be. In fact Peppe was in much greater danger than me because he dealt with them almost every day. But as he explained it to me, he'd decided that he wanted to do one worthwhile thing before he joined his Maker, and he didn't care too much about the danger. Those last few weeks when he was almost eaten up by pain he was incredibly brave.''

Beth thought about the two and a half years she had spent running from Luke. She thought about giving birth to Kristin alone in a Philadelphia city hospital. She thought about the sleazy bars where she had worked, the dreary apartments where she had lived and the endless nights of

wrenching loneliness when her whole being had cried out for
Luke. Suddenly she began to laugh.

"Oh no!" she gasped, the laughter already turning to
harsh scalding tears. "I spent two years running away from
a damned hero!" Anger welled up, choking off her sobs.
"Luke, I was your *wife*! Why didn't you tell me what was
going on?"

"Because the deputy director of the FBI told me not to!"
he shouted. He lowered his voice almost immediately, taking her hand and holding it loosely within his grasp. "No,"
he said. "That's not quite true. I didn't tell you because I
hadn't learned then that unless husbands and wives share
everything important in their lives, they eventually end up
sharing nothing at all. I had to lose you and Kristin before
I understood that marriage entails more than installing your
wife in your house and making love to her whenever you're
home."

She tightened her hold on his hand. "We both made mistakes," she said. "I had a lot to learn as well. If I'd really
trusted you, I would never have accepted that meeting at
face value. You said a little while ago that I'd already decided you were guilty before I had any evidence to back up
my fears, and you were right, Luke. I was thrown off balance by your life-style, by Cobden Farm—by all those things
that were so different from my own background. I loved you
so much and yet I couldn't seem to trust my own happiness. It was almost as if I needed to look for some problem
in our marriage, some fatal flaw that would prove we
weren't suited to each other."

A smile crinkled his eyes and softened the severe lines of
his mouth. "But we are suited to each other, aren't we,
Beth?" He drew her into his arms, and her body molded itself automatically to his. "You see? Despite everything
we've done to each other, we fit together like two halves of

one whole. Come back to Cobden Farm and be my wife again, Beth. This time we'll make it work."

She ran her hands under his sweatshirt, feeling the muscles of his back tense beneath her fingertips. She threw back her head and looked at him provocatively. "I'm not sure it would be wise for me to come," she murmured. "I think you'll have to persuade me."

He kissed the top of her nose. "How could I do that?" he asked.

"You could bribe me," she suggested.

He pretended to look shocked. "What, me? Offer a bribe?"

"Just a little one," she said. "For example, you could promise to hire me as legal advisor for your Senate campaign."

"Done. It's a deal."

Her fingers walked slowly down his spine. "Or alternatively..."

He closed his eyes. "Yes?"

"You could always take me upstairs to bed."

His eyes opened fast. He swept her into his arms and carried her up the stairs and into the bedroom. "Any suggestions about what I should do once we're in bed?"

"You should make love to me," she said promptly. "You should reduce me to a state of helpless mindless submission so that I do whatever you tell me to do."

He dropped her onto the rumpled bed and smoothed a curl out of her eyes. "Sounds easy enough," he said, "provided you give me lots of instructions." His mouth descended toward her lips and his hand moved expertly toward the zipper of her jeans. A few minutes later he lifted his head and smiled complacently as he examined her glazed eyes and moist parted lips. "How am I doing so far?"

His thumbs grazed enticingly over her nipples, and she bit back a moan of pleasure. "You seem to be getting the idea," she said thickly.

"Yes, I think I am," he agreed, a lazy smile darkening his eyes. He captured her hands and held them against the pillows, lowering his mouth and nuzzling the tiny pulse beating at the base of her throat. She writhed in gratification, and raising his head, he looked at her flushed face with sudden seriousness. "I love you, Beth," he said quietly.

Her fingers slid over his shoulders and into the thickness of his hair. "I love you, too," she whispered. "I always have, even when I tried so desperately to hate you."

"Tell me again," he commanded. "I've wanted to hear you say that so often in the past couple of years."

"I love you, Luke."

He sighed and reclaimed her mouth in a long tender kiss. His hands caressed her body, leading her expertly to the soaring joyful culmination of their lovemaking.

She was curled up in his arms, almost asleep, when she opened one exhausted eye and mumbled, "We have to buy a teddy bear."

"I know," he said. "I remember. A girl teddy bear with a yellow dress. We'll buy it this afternoon on the way home."

She smiled sleepily, her eyes already closed. "I love you, Man," she murmured. "Lots and lots."

Harlequin Presents

Coming Next Month

919 WAKING UP Amanda Carpenter
The boy next door is now the man with the golden future, while hers is still in question. What could they possibly have in common now?

920 A HIGH PRICE TO PAY Sara Craven
At the price of her mother's peace of mind and her sister's future, how can a young woman refuse to marry the one man who could give her family back everything her father lost?

921 A WORLD APART Emma Darcy
It's one thing to match wits with a fellow author on TV, quite another to be madly pursued by him in real life, where their values seem worlds apart.

922 ONE DREAM ONLY Claudia Jameson
The devastatingly attractive owner of a London toy company becomes personally interested in his new assistant. But she's afraid to risk involvement again—especially not his kind.

923 THE WADE DYNASTY Carole Mortimer
Sure, he proposed, but all he really cared about was control of the family's Alberta ranch. Still, with a family crisis reuniting them, can she deny her love for him a second time?

924 THE COUNTERFEIT SECRETARY Susan Napier
A widow tires of leading a double life—cool, efficient secretary at work, warmhearted mother of twins at home. But it's safer than falling in love with her boss, a self-proclaimed bachelor.

925 BEST LAID PLANS Rosemary Schneider
The right choice for a woman wanting marriage and children is a well-bred Boston banker, not the man with whom she shared a brief holiday romance. But love can disrupt even the best laid plans.

926 THE KISSING GAME Sally Wentworth
The new physiotherapist for a famous English soccer team expects some resistance to her appointment, but not from the youngest member of the board of directors. What could he have against her?

Available in October wherever paperback books are sold, or through Harlequin Reader Service:

In the U.S.
P.O. Box 1397
Buffalo, N.Y.
14240-1397

In Canada
P.O. Box 2800, Postal Station A
5170 Yonge Street
Willowdale, Ontario M2N 6J3

ATTRACTIVE, SPACE SAVING BOOK RACK

Display your most prized novels on this handsome and sturdy book rack. The hand-rubbed walnut finish will blend into your library decor with quiet elegance, providing a practical organizer for your favorite hard-or soft-covered books.

Only $9.95

Approximately 16" x 8" when assembled

Assembles in seconds!

To order, rush your name, address and zip code, along with a check or money order for $10.70 ($9.95 plus 75¢ postage and handling) (New York residents add appropriate sales tax), payable to *Harlequin Reader Service* to:

In the U.S.

Harlequin Reader Service
Book Rack Offer
901 Fuhrmann Blvd.
P.O. Box 1325
Buffalo, NY 14269-1325

Offer not available in Canada.

BKR-1

Where passion and destiny meet . . . there is love

Jesse's Lady

Veronica Sattler

Brianna Deveraux had a feisty spirit matched by that of only one man, Jesse Randall. In North Carolina, 1792, they dared to forge a love as vibrant and alive as life in their bold new land.

Available at your favorite bookstore in SEPTEMBER, or reserve your copy for August shipping. Send your name, address, zip or postal code with a check or money order for $5.25 (includes 75¢ for postage and handling) payable to Worldwide Library Reader Service to:

In the U.S.	In Canada
Worldwide Library	Worldwide Library
901 Fuhrmann Blvd.	P.O. Box 2800, 5170 Yonge St.
Box 1325	Postal Station A
Buffalo, New York	Willowdale, Ontario
14269-1325	M2N 6J3

PLEASE SPECIFY BOOK TITLE WITH YOUR ORDER.

JES-H-1

Harlequin Intrigue

Because romance can be quite an adventure.

Available wherever paperbacks are sold or through

Harlequin Reader Service·

In the U.S.
901 Fuhrmann Blvd.
P.O. Box 1325
Buffalo, N.Y. 14269

In Canada
P.O. Box 2800, Station "A"
5170 Yonge Street
Willowdale, Ontario M2N 6J3

INT-6R

Explore love with Harlequin in the Middle Ages, the Renaissance, in the Regency, the Victorian and other eras.

Relive within these books the endless ages of romance, set against authentic historical backgrounds. Two new historical love stories published each month.

Available starting August wherever paperback books are sold.

HIST-A-1

Could she find love as a mail-order bride?

MARIANNE WILLMAN

In the Arizona of 1873, Nora O'Shea is caught between life with a contemptuous, arrogant husband and her desperate love for Roger LeBeau, half-breed Comanche Indian scout and secret freedom fighter.

Available now at your favorite retail outlet, or order your copy by sending your name, address and zip or postal code along with a check or money order for $5.25 (includes 75¢ for postage and handling) payable to Worldwide Library Reader Service to:

In the U.S.	In Canada
Worldwide Library	Worldwide Library
901 Fuhrmann Blvd.	P.O. Box 2800, 5170 Yonge St.
Box 1325	Postal Station A
Buffalo, New York	Willowdale, Ontario
14269-1325	M2N 6J3

Please specify book title with your order.

SKY-H-1R

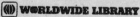 **WORLDWIDE LIBRARY**